M
E

by
DOROTHY MARTIN

MOODY PRESS
CHICAGO

© 1981 by
THE MOODY BIBLE INSTITUTE
OF CHICAGO

Library of Congress Cataloging in Publication Data

Martin, Dorothy McKay, 1921-
  Mystery of the empty house.

  SUMMARY: Two teenage girls learn what it means to
be a Christian as a result of a mystery they solve while
vacationing in the woods of Minnesota.

  [1. Mystery and detective stories. 2. Christian life—
Fiction] I. Title.

PZ7.M35682Mr   [Fic]   80-25606

ISBN 0-8024-5703-7

Printed in the United States of America

1

Vickie grabbed a towel and raced after Diane, who was already down at the edge of the lake. Diane stuck one foot into the sparkling water and then snatched it out.

"Wow, is this cold! How can the water be so icy when the sun is blazing hot? Even an unheated swimming pool is boiling compared to this."

"My dad says the water gets real cold because the lake is so deep. The water only gets warm on top, even in the hottest part of the summer."

"How can anybody swim when the water's so freezing?" Diane clutched her towel around her narrow shoulders.

Vickie laughed. "You have to jump in all at once. You'll never get up enough nerve just standing there shivering. Come on."

She dropped her towel, splashed out, ducked under and came up, shaking the water out of her eyes. Then she swam out to the floating pier that jutted into the lake. She clambered onto it and sat shivering, peering back at Diane standing at the edge of the lake, her towel wrapped around her stick figure.

"Hurry up," she yelled, motioning to Diane with a sweep of her arm. She watched Diane reluctantly drop her towel on the sandy shore, wade out into the water, and then suddenly duck under and start swimming. Soon she climbed onto the pier beside Vickie, shook her curly blond hair, and clutched her arms around her thin, trembling body, with goosebumps pebbling her arms.

"H-how d-do we g-get b-b-back? You sh-should have s-spare t-towels and a b-boat out here. I d-don't think I'll ever s-stop sh-shaking." She stared down into the water lapping against the pier. "I hate t-to think the only way to g-get b-back to shore is t-to swim."

"You ought to be fatter like I am," Vickie answered unsympathetically. "Then you wouldn't shiver so much."

"You're lucky."

"Lucky to be fat?"

"You're not fat. Anyway, you've lost weight. How much?"

"Fifteen pounds since last summer. Francine said I shouldn't lose too fast, or I might gain it all back." She looked at Diane accusingly. "You go on wolfing down hot fudge sundaes and bags of french fries and they never show on you, while I have to drink diet Cokes all the time. It's not fair."

"I still say you're lucky. Pretty soon you'll have a figure like Francine's, and I'll still be straight up and down. *That's* what's not fair!"

"I can't wait! Especially if I can be like her in other ways and snag a guy as sharp as Pete."

"Are they going to get engaged pretty soon?"

Vickie nodded. "I think so. My dad thinks Pete's terrific. And anybody he thinks is good enough for Francine has got to be practically perfect. Of course he and Pete agree on almost everything—books and politics and sports—"

"And church," Diane added as Vickie stopped abruptly.

4

"Yeah. They've got a contest going to see which one can memorize a bunch of Bible verses first."

"It's funny. Wonder why it is you don't think of someone as tall and good-looking and as sharp a dresser as Pete—and your dad—as being interested in going to church? I guess maybe it's more important than my mother thinks it is. You know she thinks your dad is kind of nuts—" Diane gave a quick glance at Vickie and said hastily, "*I* don't think that, but she says a lawyer like your dad should be smart enough to know that religion is just superstition."

Vickie looked out across the sparkling water, not answering, not saying, *My mother thinks that too, only she pretends she doesn't because she doesn't want to hurt him.*

Then Diane laughed. "I asked my mother once how come she always reads her horoscope in the paper every morning before she decides what she's going to do. Sometimes even before she decides what to wear. I asked her if that was superstition, too."

"What'd she say?"

"Got mad. Said it wasn't the same thing at all. She said something about the effect of the stars and planets on people had been proven scientifically. Oh, well. No point arguing with her."

Diane sat hugging her knees and looked around. "I still can't get over how shiny and warm the water *looks* and how cold it *feels*. This sure is different from the last time we swam in a lake."

"The last time—oh, yeah, in the Dead Sea, on spring break. One thing sure, we weren't cold that

5

day. But I like this lake better."

"You know, this is the first time I've been in a place as wild looking as this." Diane gestured around at the mass of towering trees surrounding the lake. "I've been to camps before a couple of times, but they were fancy places. They even had maid service. That's my mother's idea of camping."

She twisted to look around the circle of the lake. "I can't imagine living here all year, even through the winter, the way you said your dad's family did."

"Get him to tell you the neat story about how his great-grandparents came here. They were real pioneers. And they were brave to come here because this is supposed to be one of the wildest parts of the whole state."

"Wildest? You mean with animals?" Diane asked, her voice a mixture of excitement and alarm.

"No, with trees. See how thick and dark the woods are all around the lake?"

Diane nodded. "They grow clear down to the edge of the water all around that curve of the lake. And they're so thick they practically touch each other. It's spooky even now when the sun is shining."

She stretched out flat on her stomach on the wooden boards of the pier, her head cushioned on her folded arms.

Vickie laughed as she dribbled a handful of water along Diane's back. "Ask my dad if he thinks it's spooky. Or ask the Sullivans in that

6

house over from ours. They stay all summer and sometimes even until after Thanksgiving."

"But they've got that enormous dog to scare off anybody—"

"Who's there to scare off?" Vickie demanded.

"Well—anybody who was a—a crook and needed to hide."

"A person would be dumb to hide out here. It's too easy to get lost in these woods."

"My mother would never come here. She'd rather belong to a club with a pool and stay in the blazing hot city than have a whole lake like this where it's lonely."

"Maybe she'll let you come up with us for Christmas, and then you'll see it's not spooky, not even in the winter."

"Don't remind me of Christmas," Diane said, her voice muffled in the curve of her arm as she lay on the pier. "I can still *feel* inside me how terrible last Christmas was with Betty Lou visiting you, and the awful way I acted."

Vickie heard the shame in Diane's voice and said quickly, "I was just sitting here remembering that we didn't even know each other until just about this time last year. I didn't have any idea I'd be best friends with a smart nut like you."

Diane rolled over and sat up, laughing. "Isn't it neat?" she exclaimed. "We're so different and yet we're so alike." She squinted across at the opposite shoreline as they sat in comfortable silence. Then she asked, "What's that smoke coming up over there?"

Vickie shaded her eyes with her hand as she

looked in the direction Diane pointed. "You know I can't see that far without my glasses." She shrugged. "Probably it's someone camping."

"But it looks as though the smoke is coming right up from the trees themselves. Do you suppose it's a fire?"

"Uh-uh." Vickie nodded off to the right. "There's a forest ranger station over there. Someone's always on duty watching for fires. They have to be, up here especially. There was an awful fire once when my grandfather was a little kid."

"What happened?"

"I don't remember. You'll have to ask my dad about it. But it was real bad. People burned to death."

The thin line of white smoke spiralled gently above the tops of the thick mass of dark green pine and evergreen trees as the girls sat in the hot sun. The trunks of white birch trees grouped here and there made light stripes that gave contrast to the dark brown trunks of other trees.

"I can see why this is called Window Lake," Diane said into the comfortable silence. "Look how things are reflected in it."

She leaned over the edge of the floating pier and stared down into the clear water. Then as she sat up straight and looked out across the lake, she jerked and exclaimed, "Look at the smoke now! It's coming in bunches, Vickie, instead of in a straight line. I wish you could see it. It's like a signal!"

Her voice was an exclamation. "First there's one puff—then two right together—and now—"

She stopped, waiting breathlessly, and then said, "Aw, now it's just a thin line. In fact, I can hardly see it."

"So much for signals," Vickie said, and laughed. "One thing sure—we can't tell my folks that we—*you*—saw a smoke signal, or they might pack us up and go home, and we'll miss out on two weeks of fun. You know they get suspicious of us and our ideas. My mother would be sure we would go off and get lost in the woods."

"They have to admit we *did* figure out a mystery during spring vacation."

Vickie heard the stubborn note in Diane's voice that meant she was set for a long argument, and answered, "But my dad would say, 'One swallow doesn't make a summer.'"

"Meaning?"

"Meaning that just because we saw a mystery once when no one else did, it doesn't mean we'll find one every place we go."

Diane sighed. "The trouble is, two weeks here could be awful long if we don't find something exciting to do."

"You didn't have to come!" Vickie began indignantly, but Diane turned to her impulsively.

"I didn't mean I was bored, Vickie, honest. It was super of you to invite me along. Otherwise I'd have been stuck at my grandmother's while my mother went to New York for her vacation. My grandmother is nice, but her idea of fun is to get all dressed up and go to Marshall Fields to shop and have afternoon tea. Here with your folks I feel so—so free!" She flung out her arms.

Then she looked at Vickie. "I just meant it would be fun to have something exciting happen. You know, if we could rescue someone from almost drowning or—"

"If you plan to rescue anyone, you'll have to jump in the water faster than you did when you swam out here." Vickie ducked Diane's push and then said, "Forget that idea, because there's no one here to rescue from anything. My mother's a super swimmer. The people in the other houses are mostly adults. There used to be lots of families with kids who came summers when I was real little, but not so many come anymore."

She looked at Diane, whose eyes were focused on the distant trees on the opposite shore. "Can you still see smoke?"

Diane shook her head. Then she asked abruptly, "Have you ever walked clear around the lake? Can a person go all the way around?"

"I haven't. Not all the way. But my dad has."

"How far is it?"

"I think my dad said ten miles—maybe twelve. Mostly you can walk right along the shore. But some places you have to wind up through the trees because there isn't any ground to walk on. The trees grow clear down to the water. We can walk around it if you want to."

"Tomorrow?" Diane's voice jumped with eagerness.

"OK by me." Then, doubtfully, she added, "Ten miles is a long way—"

"But if you figure we can walk a mile in about twenty minutes—"

"*Twenty* minutes?"

"MmHmm. My—uh, my—dad—" She stopped, shot Vickie a quick glance, and after a minute went on. "My dad figured it out for me once when he was being—was being—friendly. We walked a mile once from our house to a park. We stayed at the park for a while and he—he pushed me on the swings." Her voice drifted off, and she finished in a whisper, "I think I was about six."

Vickie sat in the bright sun, her arms around her bare knees, not looking at Diane, but hearing the wistfulness of her voice as she reached far back for a stray, happy memory of her father. And she thought again how lucky she was to have Carl Montgomery for her father instead of Roger Stewart.

Then Diane moved abruptly and stood up. "So, if it's ten miles around, and we figure twenty minutes to a mile—"

"Hey, wait," Vickie objected. "Walking a mile on a straight, even sidewalk is a lot different from getting tangled up in bushes and climbing over logs and detouring around trees."

"I hadn't thought of that. Well, let's see. If we figure two miles an hour instead of three, we could make it in five hours." She stopped, frowning in thought, and then burst out impulsively, "Oh, Vickie, I bet we could make it faster than we think! We could go right after breakfast and take a lunch. That'd be fun."

"OK," Vickie agreed and stood up, stretching. "I'm ready to go back now. You coming?"

Diane nodded, but stood still, looking out across the water. "I wish we could figure out how far into the woods the fire was that we saw."

"We didn't see any fire—only smoke. And remember, only you saw it."

"Yeah, but if there's smoke, there's fire. And I *did* see it."

"What I mean is, it wasn't a *fire* fire—something dangerous."

"How can you tell?" Diane argued.

"I think if it was a real fire the smoke would have been black. And more of it. And would have lasted longer." She watched Diane put her hands up to each side of her face and then stretch her arms straight out in front of her. "Now what?"

"I'm trying to figure out where the smoke was from where we are. It was right in line with that row of white trees over there, those—what kind are they?"

"Birch."

"Yeah, right behind them."

"We don't know how far behind," Vickie argued. "It could be miles and miles. My dad says it's hard to estimate distances when you're in the woods. He says people get lost in the woods, unless they have a compass, because all the trees look alike and it's easy to get turned around. Whatever you saw could have been way in. Too far for us to go."

"But maybe it wasn't. Maybe it's closer to the lake than you think. Maybe we'll be able to see the place tomorrow when we walk around. Wouldn't it be neat if we could do a Smokey the

Bear job and warn someone about putting out campfires? Maybe there's a dumb Boy Scout troop out there."

Vickie laughed. "I'm sure a Scout leader would appreciate our barging in to give advice. What was it your mother called you once? An incorrigible snoop?"

Vickie fell into the water as Diane shoved her, and she surfaced, shaking water from her face as she looked up at Diane still standing on the pier.

"You're as bad as I am," Diane answered. "I bet you think those were smoke signals too, only you're not admitting it."

"OK. Tomorrow we'll look when we walk by *if* we can see anything from the edge of the lake. But in the meantime we don't say anything to my folks."

"Agreed. The only thing I'm going to say about fires is to ask your dad about the one you said happened here before. I'd like to know if it burned the whole town and where it happened. Do you suppose if we dug around we'd be able to find traces of a lost civilization?"

Vickie shook her head, as she treaded water and laughed. "Lost civilization in the middle of Minnesota? A great archaeologist you are!"

"Well, I've got to start someplace," Diane retorted.

"I'll race you back to shore. All I'm interested in digging up right now is a sandwich. I'm starved."

2

Vickie felt the sweat trickling down her face and her glasses sliding down her nose. She was hot from the exertion of climbing over fallen trees and through overgrown weeds and low, prickly bushes, and from plodding through layers of sand along the shore.

"Wait a sec," Diane called. "Gotta tie my shoelace. One of 'em is broken, and it's so short it keeps coming untied."

"OK by me. I want to sit down a minute anyway." Wiping her forehead, Vickie sank down on a log. "How long do you suppose we've been walking?"

"I don't know. What time do you think it is? It was dumb of us *both* to forget our watches."

Vickie squinted up at the sun. "I'm no good at telling time by where the sun is, are you?"

"I've never done it, but I've read how people do it. What you do is look at where the sun is. When it's right overhead, it's noon. Then as it gets later and the sun goes down, you can figure the time from the slant of the sun."

"OK, so what's the slant now?"

Diane frowned as she shaded her eyes with one hand and stared up into the sky. "Well, let's see. We left about ten o'clock? The sun's still pretty high. You think it's about noon?"

"So we've been walking two hours and that means we've come—" Vickie stopped, and then said, *"If* we made a mile in twenty minutes like

14

you said we could, then we've come——"

"Six miles." Diane's voice was sharp with impatience at Vickie's fumbling math. "There are three twenty-minutes in an hour. So two hours makes six miles."

"But we said we couldn't go that fast. Looks to me like we still have at least halfway to go."

"Maybe it's more than ten miles around," Diane suggested. She stood up and looked around the expanse of shoreline and nodded. "You're right. We're only about halfway."

"I think we've been walking too slow," Vickie said. "And detouring too much. When you lead, you keep getting away from the edge of the lake and too far up in the woods. And it's so much harder walking there. If we stay right here at the edge, there's not as much stuff to climb over and around and get stuck in. It'll be bad enough when we do get into all those trees on the curve over there."

"Yeah, but staying along the shore isn't as interesting," Diane protested.

Vickie turned to face her, hands on her hips as she said accusingly, "That's not the reason you've been fooling around and stopping so often to tie your shoelace. You're still thinking about the smoke you saw yesterday. You think someone's in the woods sending a signal, and you want to detour and find out. That's the reason you suggested this walk in the first place."

Diane grinned. "Sure," she admitted cheerfully.

"You broke your shoelace on purpose so you'd

15

have an excuse to stop and look around. I know that lace was OK this morning because I grabbed your shoes out of the closet by mistake and both shoelaces were OK then."

"Sure," Diane said again. "I didn't want to say let's go look, because I didn't think you were going along with me on the idea that the smoke *might* mean something. Something more than just being smoke, I mean."

"*I* do," Vickie retorted. "It's my folks who won't, and you know it." She looked around, kicking at the dry ground and the fallen leaves that rustled underfoot as they inched along over the shore where the sand had been eroded. "I'm sure you saw smoke yesterday. But you know what my dad said when you told him."

She stopped and turned to face Diane again, her voice still accusing. "We weren't going to say anything to my dad, remember?"

"It just slipped out, Vickie," Diane protested. "Anyway, he said if there had been a fire, an open fire, the forest ranger would have raised an alarm because of the woods being so dry."

"But what if the fire was in a house, coming out of a chimney? That's legal, isn't it? That's not dangerous."

"The ranger would have checked that out too, to be sure it was OK. And anyway, I don't think there's any house way deep in the woods. Nobody would build a house way in here. People want to be close to shore so they won't have to go so far to swim."

They had stopped to rest again, panting from

16

the effort of pushing through tangling underbrush and fallen trees.

"It looks like a jungle," Diane said. "I can't imagine people really living here at all. How long ago did your dad say people moved away?"

"About the time of the First World War. So many men had to go and fight that the women couldn't keep up the farms. Anyway, I told you there weren't all that many people living here—"

Vickie stopped and looked at Diane. "You asked me and then you didn't listen."

"I'm sorry. I was just looking around, trying to figure out—you know, where we are—"

"You mean where we are according to where the smoke was."

Diane nodded. "Vickie—why don't we plow through the woods just a little way? We won't go very far, especially if we don't see anything right away."

Vickie looked around, frowning doubtfully. "Well—Dad always used to warn Francine and me about getting lost if we wandered too far away from things we recognized."

"That's just it, we wouldn't." Diane's eyes sparkled. "Look, let's do this the way we would if we were explorers coming here for the first time. We can leave a trail—"

"Oh, sure," Vickie nodded. "Like Hansel and Gretel. Did you bring a dry piece of bread along to crumble? Or do we divvy up a sandwich?"

"I'm serious!" Diane protested. She reached for the red scarf tied around her forehead. "We can tear my scarf into—"

"So *that's* why you wore it! When you said athletes wore something like that to keep the sweat out of their eyes, I wondered why you didn't wear a white one, because that looks so hot. You wore a red one on purpose."

Diane grinned. "Sure. Red shows up better. We can tear it up and tie strips to the trees as we go along and then follow them back."

She looked at the doubt that still showed in the expression on Vickie's face and insisted, "I'm sure the smoke came from straight through here. Look." She pointed back toward the floating pier in front of the Montgomery house and then at the group of birch trees near where they stood. "Remember yesterday we—I—figured the smoke came from somewhere behind these white tree trunks? Aren't these the same trees?"

Vickie followed the direction of Diane's pointing finger and nodded slow agreement. "OK, let's try. But if we don't find anything in—what?—fifteen minutes?—we'll come back."

They tore the thin scarf into narrow strips. Diane tied one around the slender trunk of a white birch and then pushed her way past it, stepping over low bushes and tangled vines, with Vickie close behind her. Diane stopped and looked back over her shoulder. "Can you see it?"

Vickie shook her head. "No. I'm going back and tie the strip higher on the tree. If a bear came along he could pull it right off."

Diane stopped abruptly. "A bear? You're kidding, aren't you? There aren't bears in here, are there?"

"I wouldn't be going along with your crazy idea if I thought there were," Vickie retorted. "I'm dumb, but not that dumb."

"Vickie!" Hurt was evident in Diane's voice. "I don't think this is crazy. Maybe the forest ranger didn't see the smoke, and we'd be doing a good deed if we found someone being careless about a fire."

"And since you're naturally snoopy—" Vickie ducked the glob of dirt Diane lobbed at her and said, "OK, OK, I'm kidding. Go ahead."

Diane crashed through the underbrush, stopping every so often to tie a strip of the bright red scarf high around a tree trunk. Vickie kept trying to estimate the time.

Finally she said, "I'd say it's been about twenty minutes since we started this, and we haven't seen anything but trees and these horrible scratchy bushes that keep tripping me up. And mosquitoes and gnats. I think we'd better give up and go back."

"Let's just go until the last strip of scarf is used up," Diane begged. "I've got only two more pieces."

"OK."

To avoid being hit by the tree branches that whipped back as Diane pushed her way through, Vickie followed several feet behind. Diane tied the next to the last piece of scarf on a tree and called, "I'm going to take twenty giant steps and tie the last strip."

"You can't," Vickie called back. "You didn't say 'Mother, may I!'"

19

Diane laughed. "OK, 'Mother, may I?'" She began counting out loud.

Vickie watched Diane's figure as she took huge steps forward and on the tenth count was lost from sight. She stopped to shake sand out of one shoe, lost her balance, and sat down hard. She got up to follow the faint sound of Diane's voice as she counted, "Nineteen—and—twenty."

The twenty seemed to linger in the air, repeating itself over and over in a sudden silence that followed Diane's voice. Vickie caught up with Diane as Diane stood motionless and peered past a fringe of trees where the thick forest jungle had thinned.

"Diane—"

"Shh!" Diane cut off her voice with an abrupt gesture.

"What is it?" Vickie whispered and then said, "Oh!" as she looked where Diane pointed.

They stood on the edge of what must once have been a lawn that sloped toward them, ground that was now thickly covered by underbrush. Across the clearing stood a large house, a hill looming behind it. It was a two-story house, and the row of windows in the upper level stared back at them like sightless eyes. Nothing stirred in the silence of the woods; no smoke poured from the chimney to indicate life.

Vickie shivered as she stared at the silent house. "It's spooky, Diane. Let's go."

"Didn't you know there was a house here? Haven't you ever seen it?"

"No. I've never been this far along the lake and never this far into the woods. I told you my dad always warned us we could get lost—"

"Yeah, but this is such a big house. Someone must have lived here once."

"My dad probably knows something about it. Come *on,* let's go."

"Vickie—wait a minute. As long as we've come this far, let's at least go up and look at it—"

"Diane! Are you crazy? I don't want to go any closer."

"Why not? You can tell the house is empty. Nothing could hurt us."

"Let's wait," Vickie pleaded nervously. "Let's ask my dad if he knows who used to live here."

"Well—OK—" Diane half turned, her voice trailing off in regret. She stopped to look back over her shoulder. "Let me go up and look in one of the windows. I just want to see what it looks like inside. I bet once it was a really neat place. And it sure looks empty."

"But if this *is* where the smoke came from, maybe it isn't empty. Maybe someone is there just keeping quiet."

"I won't go inside. And we can run if we see or hear anything."

Without waiting for Vickie's objections, Diane moved cautiously from the shelter of the trees out into the clearing, stepping high over the weeds and vines and small clumps of wild grass. Nothing stirred in the silence as she walked toward the house.

Vickie held her breath as she watched Diane move slowly toward the porch and stand for a moment at the first sagging wooden step. Then, as she lifted her foot to step up, a low moaning sound suddenly came from nowhere and yet from everywhere, completely surrounding them.

Diane turned and raced back toward Vickie, and they both dashed headlong through the dense woods, stumbling over fallen logs and slipping and sliding over weeds and bushes.

Vickie's throat ached as she gasped for breath in the wild plunge for safety. Tree branches whipped against them, catching and snarling their hair, and bushes scratched their legs. Neither one stopped or looked behind until they broke through the woods and stood panting for breath at the edge of the lake, glad to be in the warm sunlight.

They dropped onto the sandy shore, exhausted and trembling with the relief of being safe.

Diane swallowed hard as her gasping breath forced out words. "Wh-what—was—that?"

"I—don't—know," Vickie answered.

"It didn't—sound—like an—animal."

Vickie shook her head. She took a deep breath, forcing herself to relax. "Anyway, we *both* heard it, so we know it was *something*."

"That means if there are no wild animals in here, then the noise was made by someone, by a person, even if we didn't see or hear anyone. That means the noise has got to be connected with the smoke we saw."

Vickie sat listening to Diane's building up of facts. Then as she looked around them, she burst out laughing.

"Look," she answered Diane's questioning stare. She waved her arm around. "Look where

22

we are. We're way down along the lake from where we went into the woods."

"So?"

"Well, look. We carefully tied all those strips of cloth to the trees so we could have a trail back and not get lost. Then when we heard the noise we didn't even think of them. We just turned and ran and crashed our way out. We were both too scared to stop and think."

"I wasn't scared," Diane protested indignantly. "I just ran because you did."

"Yeah? Then how come you were way ahead of me when we got out here, even though I had a head start because you were clear up by the house?"

"Because I'm a faster runner," Diane answered. Then she grinned. "You're right. I was scared. That noise came so suddenly and sounded so close, I felt sure someone was going to reach out and grab me any minute."

"And we lost our lunch, too," Vickie moaned. "It's way back somewhere in the woods. We'd better go home and not try to go all the way around the lake today."

"I'm ready."

"If you're giving up so easy, it proves you really didn't intend to walk around. You only suggested doing it to get this far. I hope you're satisfied!"

"Of course," Diane answered cheerfully. "Now that we know there's a house there, we can come back and look at it again. Do you think your dad would come with us?"

"Maybe we can talk him into coming tomorrow."

"I kind of think I'd feel braver with him along," Diane admitted.

3

"So this is your marked trail back," Mr. Montgomery teased as he looked at the strips of red cloth turned from perky signals into limp, stringy rags by last night's crashing rain storm.

"We thought we needed them to show us how to get back," Vickie answered. "Only when we heard that noise, we just turned and ran. I didn't even stop to think whether we were going in the right direction. All I wanted to do was to get away."

Mr. Montgomery nodded. "You showed good sense to leave a trail even though you didn't follow it back. It's easy to panic, and that's why I've warned against wandering around in these woods. I've tried to follow that advice myself. People have been lost in dense woods like this for weeks because they scared easily." He stopped, a grin lighting his face. "It's easy to panic even at imaginary noises."

"Dad! You didn't hear it!"

"It was *real*," Diane insisted.

"Well, so are owls and squirrels and bears—"

"Bears!" Diane, in front, stopped so suddenly that Vickie collided with her. "Vickie said there weren't any bears."

Her voice ended with a high squeak, and Mr. Montgomery laughed as he shook his head. "No, not anymore. There were at one time, of course. In fact, my great-grandmother killed a bear once right at her back door. But you probably heard an owl or a racoon or a—"

"Do they sound like this?" Diane demanded. She again imitated the sound she had made last night, when they had poured out the story while they helped him repaint the rowboat.

"Decidedly not. But I'm not willing to see spooks behind every tree. There is usually a logical explanation for almost everything that happens."

"The logical explanation for this noise is that someone made it," Diane said, her voice stubborn.

"Diane," said Vickie suddenly, "what if, when we get to where we saw the house, it isn't there? I saw a mystery movie on TV once like that, where a house was there, and then when the people went back it was gone."

"Well, *I* know we did see it. We saw the house, and we heard a noise. And in just a couple of minutes I'll prove it."

Diane half ran a few yards, stumbling over weeds and logs, and said, "See? There it is. Just the way we saw it yesterday."

Her voice and face were triumphant as she gestured through the thin fringe of trees that bordered the partially cleared space, and turned to look up at Mr. Montgomery.

"Well, well." He stood with his hands in his pockets and stared at the house, with the row of windows in the upper story staring back at them, unblinking.

Looking at the house, Vickie saw details she had not noticed yesterday. "Look how it's built, Diane. That low, one-story part at this end looks like it's just tacked on to the two-story part."

"Sort of like an attached garage, only it isn't a garage," Diane added.

"The low part likely was the original house and then the bigger part was built later." As he moved across the clearing, Mr. Montgomery got tangled in the matted underbrush that covered the ground. He stood in front of the worn boards of the sagging steps that led up to the porch.

"The smoke we saw could have come from the chimney." Diane pointed to it as she and Vickie followed him to stand by the steps.

"That could be," Mr. Montgomery nodded. "Chimneys usually stay in usable condition for years."

"You knew this house was here?" Diane turned to him in surprise.

"Well, not exactly." He frowned, seeming puzzled. "I knew there had once been a house back in here somewhere. But I didn't know it was still standing in such good condition."

"Such *good* condition!" Vickie echoed.

"For its age, yes." He frowned again, studying the house. "I'm trying to remember—"

"Can't we go inside?" Diane interrupted, her usual impatience sending her jumping up and down.

"I don't see why not," he answered. "I don't imagine the door locks anymore."

The girls followed him, stepping hesitantly up the broken steps and across the porch. The door creaked in protest as Mr. Montgomery pushed it open and gestured with his hand for the girls to enter.

27

"You go first, Dad."

"Yeah, we'll follow you," Diane echoed.

Vickie was glad that Diane was nervous too, and both of them walked close behind Mr. Montgomery. The inside was dark, because grimy windows dimmed the brilliant outdoor sunlight. It took a few minutes to adjust to the changed light.

"It *is* empty!" Diane's voice in the bare room carried her disappointed relief.

Mr. Montgomery smiled at her. "I can't resist an 'I told you so.' "

Vickie sniffed. "What's that funny smell?"

"Probably mustiness from the place being empty and closed up. And from dirt also."

"Who used to live here, Mr. Montgomery?"

"I will have to look up some history of the area to be able to answer you definitely. For now, let me see what kind of detectives you are. Look around and decide from what you see who you think lived here. Now remember, we are a long way from town and a long way from other houses. Our house is probably the closest, and you know how far we walked."

"Why would anyone build a house way out here?" Diane's voice was puzzled. "There isn't any road to it, is there?"

"Keep in mind that the surroundings have changed over the years. This house was not always quite this isolated."

"But even so it must have been lonely for whoever lived here." Vickie shivered a little in the musty dimness.

"Haven't you read about people who felt

28

crowded if their nearest neighbors were twenty miles away—" Mr. Montgomery began.

"Oh, you mean the Daniel Boone type," Diane interrupted.

Mr. Montgomery nodded and then gestured around. "All right now. What do you see?"

"Well, I think once this was a nice house," Vickie answered. "Look at the staircase going up to the second floor. Some of the spokes or whatever you call them, are broken and so are some of the steps. But look how they curve around. It looks so—what's that word?—elegant. And the rooms are big and probably are sunny when the windows are clean."

"It's not very sunny out here," Diane called from where she had disappeared through another door, her voice muffled by distance. "Come look—here's something funny."

"What?" Pushing through a door into what had once been a kitchen, Vickie and her father followed the sound of Diane's voice.

"Look," Diane answered. "See how dark it is on this side of the room? And how light it is on that side? I wonder how come one side has windows and the other doesn't?"

Vickie scraped dirt from the inside of one window and tried to peer out. "It's because that side is built right against the hill and this side isn't. That side is the one-story tacked-on part. I wonder why they built that side almost as though it's part of the hill?"

She directed the question to her father, who walked along the dark half of the room, his lips puckered in the soundless whistle he always had when he was thinking hard about something. He knocked along the paneled wall at various places, listening each time to the sound. Then he ran his hand slowly up and down the wall, pushing on it.

"Dad? How come you're doing that?"

"Oh, I'm just curious. As to the question you just asked, remember that people who came to settle new parts of the country often had to build a temporary shelter quickly. This was pretty wild country at one time. There were a lot of Indians who were not too eager for white men to settle on their land. I imagine whoever built this did it quickly and against the hill for two reasons— warmth and safety."

"Safety? Oh, so they only had to watch for Indian attacks from the front and sides, not the back?"

"That's right."

"You mean this house was built *that* long ago?" Diane's face lit up with eagerness.

"Wait, wait." Mr. Montgomery held up his hands in protest. "I'm only speculating. However, I am curious about the place. It would be interesting to see if we can track down some information about the house. I wonder—"

"What?" The girls spoke together, watching his abstracted look as he seemed to be measuring distances in his mind. He went back to the wooden wall on the side by the hill and again pressed up and down at various places.

Then he turned and asked, "What else have you deduced about the place?"

Vickie looked around. "Seems funny to have paneling on kitchen walls. Only it's not really paneling like in our den. The wall has grooves down it, but the wood isn't smooth."

"This table is awful rickety, and so are these two chairs." Diane rubbed her hand over the table. "Ugh, it's dirty. Anna would have a fit."

Mr. Montgomery laughed. "Or else she'd have a marvelous time cleaning."

Vickie pulled open a cupboard door. "Here are a couple of plates and cups. Three forks, but only one rusty knife. Oh, and a couple of spoons." She picked up one of the plates, absently running her fingers over it as she turned to watch Diane cautiously push wide a door that opened off the kitchen.

"I thought the bedrooms would be upstairs. But here are two—beds?" Her voice rose in a question. "I've never seen any like these. They've got—what do you call these coiled-up things under the mattress?"

"Springs," Mr. Montgomery answered. "Beds used to be made like that."

"Well," Diane said, frowning around the barren, dust-blanketed room. "You can tell no one lives here. But then who made the noise we heard?"

"I guess maybe it was an animal of some kind," Vickie said. "It just seemed loud and scary because we weren't expecting to hear anything. We just ran without waiting to figure out what it really was."

"Maybe—". Diane dragged the word out reluctantly.

"Another proof that you didn't see smoke the other day, at least not coming from this chimney, is right in front of your eyes."

"Where?"

Mr. Montgomery nodded at the fireplace. "Show me again how good your powers of deduction are."

The girls walked over and squatted down in front of the fireplace. "I don't see anything," Vickie said over her shoulder.

"That's just it," her father replied. "All you see is the dirt and grime and debris that would just naturally accumulate over time even if the fireplace were not used."

"I get it," Diane exclaimed. "You mean there's nothing to show that there was a fire in it a couple of days ago."

"Exactly."

"But maybe whoever used it cleaned it up," she objected.

"Well then it would be cleaner than this. There wouldn't be dirt here at all, I suppose," Vickie suggested.

"But maybe whoever made that fire wasn't smart enough to think of that," Diane argued.

Mr. Montgomery laughed as he walked toward the door. "I give up. You two knew you were going to be here for two weeks and couldn't stand the thought of no excitement. All right, go ahead. I won't stop you from playing up your supposed mystery."

Diane stood looking wistfully up the stairs. "Can't we go up and see what it's like up there?"

"No. Those stairs look pretty decrepit. I think we've snooped in the past enough for one day."

He held the door open, motioning them out, and watched them as they reluctantly followed. He pulled the door firmly behind him. "I am going to play the stern parent and forbid you to prowl around this old place by yourselves."

"How come? If there's no one here—"

"Yeah, Mr. Montgomery. No one lives here. And you said yourself the noise wasn't made by anyone—"

"My warning is very serious, girls, and I want you to obey it. This is such an isolated spot. A tree could fall on you, and your shouts might not be heard for hours."

"But, Dad, we'd be careful. Besides, a tree wouldn't fall on both of us at the same time."

Mr. Montgmery stopped as he plunged through the woods and turned to face them. "Vickie! Diane!"

The tone of his voice warned them against anymore arguing. After a minute Diane grinned. "That's where the 'Children, obey your parents' fits, huh?"

Vickie saw her father's surprised look and was sure it was reflected on her own face. She was sure those words were from the Bible, but she hadn't known that Diane knew them.

Diane had already changed the subject, exclaiming, "These branches keep grabbing my curls and getting my hair all tangled. I had an awful time combing it last night."

"I wish there were some better way back to our

house without having to plow through the woods every time," Vickie complained. "I get tangled in the weeds, and my legs get all scratched."

"Remember, this is the last time you will do this, at least by yourselves." Mr. Montgomery's voice was a stern reminder. Then he added, "When we get out of the woods to the shore, I'm going to jog on ahead. I promised to barbeque dinner this evening so your mother can keep at the painting she is working on."

"What's it of? If it's something you can recognize, you'll be glad," Vickie teased.

"True. But then, I've always admitted that your mother has better eyesight than I do. That makes her able to see shapes and meanings that I can't in those wild canvases of hers. And don't forget that she sells quite a few of the paintings that are incomprehensible to me."

"Does she ever paint things like—well, like the lake for example? With real trees like these?" Diane gestured around.

"You haven't looked at the one she started soon after we arrived Saturday?" Mr. Montgomery questioned. When the girls shook their heads he explained. "She is doing a lake scene now. She told me she was going to do a picture for my birthday and asked if I had a preference. I suggested a scene of the lake. There's a good place in my office for it."

"What if she does it in purples and hot pinks?" Vickie teased.

He shook his head. "No. She knows how much this lake means to me. I have roots here that go back several generations. Her picture will be one that I can sit back and look at on gloomy winter days and see trees reflected in the lake and the sun shimmering on the water and feel the peace of this place. The picture will bring back happy memories from past years when I came here every summer to visit my grandparents."

"Tell Diane about your grandparents and everybody who first came here. I told her we had relatives who were pioneers just like those we see on TV programs."

He nodded. "They were. The story goes back to my father's great-grandfather who came to this country from England. That's where the Montgomery name comes from. Somewhere along the way he met a family who were coming to live with relatives who had already settled in Minnesota. He fell in love with the oldest daughter and followed her here to marry her."

"But they were from Sweden, weren't they?" Vickie asked.

"Yes. They came to Minnesota because they had heard the climate and surroundings were similar to what they were used to in the old country. It kept them from being too homesick for their old familiar life. It was a struggle even to survive at first. But they managed to put down roots until this became home for them—and for the rest of us who came along for several generations."

Diane, following behind them, had listened silently. Then she said, "You're all lucky."

She glanced up at Mr. Montgomery as he half-turned and answered the question in his eyes. "I mean to belong someplace where lots of people before you belonged. My mother and I—" She lifted her shoulders in a slight movement. "We don't belong to the past anywhere."

Vickie walked along in the silence that followed Diane's voice with its shadings of anger and longing and hurt. Diane's father must not have bothered to answer the letter she had written him when they got home from Israel. She remembered Diane's brief "I guess he didn't get my present. At least he hasn't written to say so." Her voice had sounded unconcerned to cover the hurt.

Then she heard her father's quiet voice. "The past isn't nearly as important as the present, Diane. No one can control the past to make it better or worse. But each one of us can do something about the present and future."

He stopped as they came out of the gloom of the woods to the sunny shore. With a note of laughter in his voice, he added, "As usual I can back that with a quotation from the Bible. It's a thought from the New Testament that is somewhat long and involved, so let me summarize it for you. The man who wrote it was a brilliant man named Paul. I suppose at one time he was rich as well as being extremely well educated. But when he became a follower of Christ, he said he left behind all his goals and ambitions and connections of the past. He was only concerned with reaching his goal of knowing Jesus Christ better every day."

Vickie shot him a quick glance. She still felt uncomfortable when he talked about the Bible, even though he did it in a natural way and it al-

36

ways seemed to fit whatever the conversation was about. She turned with a startled look as Diane asked, "That's what you're trying to do, isn't it?"

She saw her father nod, his face sober. "I hope that is true of me, Diane. I hope people can tell that Jesus Christ is the center of my life."

Then with a sudden shift of mood, he gave each of them a playful shove and said, "I've changed my mind about going on ahead. I'll give you girls a head start and race you home. You get going, and I'll count to five before I start. Go on."

They raced off along the shore, kicking up puffs of sand as they ran. From behind them Mr. Montgomery shouted, "The goal is to touch your mother's chair without disturbing her concentration."

Vickie won by putting on a burst of speed right at the end, stretching to touch the canvas back of the chair where her mother sat in the sunny yard.

Her mother turned to look at them, wiping her hands on a cloth, and exclaimed, "Why are you running so hard on such a hot day?"

"Dad—was—racing us," Vickie answered in gulps of breath.

"You had better all sit down and cool off."

"Did you finish? Do I get a look at my gift soon, or must I wait until my birthday?" Mr. Montgomery put his arm around her shoulders as he asked, and he looked at the easel with the painting facing away from them.

"I am not quite through, but I believe I will let you see it anyway. Since it's *your* lake and *your* trees, you should have the privilege of suggesting changes. But remember, I can't put in what's not there."

37

She turned to the girls. "Scoot in and get the pitcher of lemonade from the refrigerator. Bring extra ice," she called after them as they clattered up the steps to the screened porch.

"Come look," Mr. Montgomery called as they came back. Vickie was carrying a tray with glasses and ice, and Diane brought the frosted pitcher of lemonade. "It's terrific. Just what I wanted."

Vickie stared at the painting. "Look!" she exclaimed, just as Diane said, "Hey, you got the smoke in."

Mrs. Montgomery looked bewildered. "The smoke?"

"Right there. Coming up behind those trees."

"How come you put it in?" Vickie demanded.

"Because it was there," her mother retorted. "You know I paint only what I see. If there had not been smoke in the sky the day I painted that part, it would not be in the picture."

"What day was it you painted it?" Diane asked, excitement squeaking her voice.

"Oh, I don't know," Mrs. Montgomery shrugged in answer. "Yesterday—no, the day before. Let's see, that would have been Sunday. Yes, I started it Saturday soon after we arrived and worked on that thick background of trees that day and the next."

"But not today?" Vickie asked.

"Do you see smoke today?" she answered, gesturing toward the shining lake. Then she looked at them. "What is this about? What difference does it make whether the smoke is there today or any other day?"

"Let me have a chance to ask a question, girls." He turned to his wife. "Louise, did you hear the girls ask me yesterday whether there was a cabin or house over in that general direction because they had seen smoke spiraling up over the trees?"

"If I did, I didn't pay any attention. I may have. Why?"

"Well, if you heard us discussing it, you might have been unconsciously influenced to paint in smoke."

"Carl, you know I paint only what I actually see."

"But Dad says you have better eyesight than anyone else and so you paint things no one else can see."

Vickie tried to keep a straight face as she spoke, but laughed as her mother reached to swipe a streak of blue paint down her cheek.

"That may be true when I'm doing *my* kind of painting. But when I do a landscape, I'm a literalist. Nothing goes in that is not there. So there would not be smoke in this picture if I had not actually seen it that day."

She stopped to look at the three of them standing in a semicircle, Vickie's and Diane's faces alive with excitement, and Mr. Montgomery's forehead lined in a frown.

"OK, Dad. Now what do you think? *Did* we see smoke or not?"

Mr. Montgomery looked at the painting and then away across to the dark woods from which they had just come.

"I think I had better have a talk with the forest ranger tomorrow."

4

Mr. Montgomery shoved his chair back from the breakfast table on the screened porch, crossed his legs, and held up his cup for the coffee Mrs. Montgomery poured. He looked at Vickie and Diane, who had swallowed strawberries and cold cereal, gulped down french toast, rushed to brush their teeth, and who now sat impatiently waiting for him to get the day started.

He smiled apologetically at them. "If you will give me time to finish this one cup of coffee, I'll promise not to drink another."

"I can't wait to see what a forest ranger place looks like!" Vickie exclaimed.

Her father held up a hand. "I've been thinking, girls. I have an idea it would be profitable to investigate something else first this morning. I'd like you to come along."

"Sure," Diane answered promptly. "Where?"

"I'd like to check out some records that might give us a clue to that old house. The nearest place is the courthouse in the city, which is about an hour's drive from here. We may want to go to the library there, too."

"Can't we go to the forest ranger's first?" Vickie's voice showed her impatience.

"I think Diane will veto that idea when I explain the purpose of the trip in more detail."

"Why me?"

"Because we're going to be archaeologists."

"Hey, neat! But I thought archaeology was digging stuff up."

"It is. And that is exactly what we are going to do—dig stuff up, as you put it. Not from the ground, however. We'll be digging into old papers and books and finding things that way."

He reached behind him to a chair next to the buffet and picked up a large brown leather book with the words Holy Bible lettered in faded gold across the front cover.

"Wow, that looks heavy." Diane reached across the table to trace the letters with one finger.

"I rummaged around up in the attic last night before I went to bed, remembering I had seen this once long ago. You see, in the years before people were born in hospitals, and before the government insisted on giving us all Social Security numbers, people kept a record in the family Bible of births and marriages and deaths. This one belonged to my great-grandparents. It's got my name in it. See?"

He flipped to the middle of the book and showed the pages where names were listed in columns labeled Births, Marriages, Deaths.

"There I am. My name was in God's Book all this time, and I didn't know it." He sat silent, his eyes looking beyond the others and out the windows.

Vickie watched him from where she sat on the railing, which ran the length of the screened porch, and thought about how neat he was. He always had been. Yet—since last April, since what had happened to him in Israel, he was even nicer and

41

happier and gentler than he had been all her life. Vickie remembered the low-toned conversation she had heard between her mother and Francine.

"What happened to Dad over there?" Francine had asked. "I've always known I had the best father in the world, but now he's even better. Is that what accepting Christ as Savior means? Pete said it is. He says it makes bad people good and good people better—or anyway, it's supposed to."

Her mother's voice, low, faintly troubled, had answered, "Yes, there is an inner change in him, a new depth. A—a luster."

When Vickie had looked up that last word in the dictionary, the first definition was "shining by reflecting light" and the second was "radiance of beauty."

She looked at her father. He was not beautiful, but he was certainly handsome and athletic and terrific. Once again she felt sorry for Diane, whose only memories of her father hurt because they were bitter.

She came back to the present when Diane jumped restlessly from the chair by the table. "I can't wait to get started! What do you think we'll find out about that house?"

"Maybe nothing," he answered.

"But you said—"

"Wait a minute, now. All that I have stirring at the back of my mind someplace is a long ago memory. My grandfather once made some reference to a house somewhere in the area that was rumored to have been part of the Underground Railroad—"

"Oh, we know about *that*," Diane broke in, her voice excited. "It wasn't really a railroad, but people who helped slaves escape from the South and come north."

But Mrs. Montgomery interrupted, shaking her head, her forehead creased in doubt. "But surely the Underground Railroad was not this far north, Carl. If I remember history, the Underground Railroad was active before and during the Civil War."

"Many of the slaves headed for safety in Canada, so some would have come this far. Whether through here, of course, I don't know."

"Yes, but any house here built that long ago would surely not still be standing, Carl."

"Remember how old this house is," he reminded her. "Older than my grandfather." He laughed then, embarrassed. "I'm being as quick as the girls to look for a mystery. Still, that house *is* old—and my grandfather *did* say—" He stood up. "We'd better get started looking for answers. Louise, do you want to come?"

She shook her head. "No. I'm going to be lazy, and may even let my painting rest. I think I will simply stretch out in the sun after a swim. With all you have planned for the day, I won't have to think of getting you lunch."

She waved at them as Mr. Montgomery backed the car out of the driveway.

"Now don't get your hopes up," he cautioned as he drove along the highway. "We may not find the kind of records we need. The terrible fire that swept through just west of here created a great deal

43

of confusion. People barely saved themselves and their livestock. They had no time to think of other belongings, not even pictures. So naturally records of past events were probably lost. I understand that even the courthouse in the city suffered some fire damage."

"Well, anyway, no matter what we find out about the house in the past, that won't help solve the mystery about the smoke—"

"You mean your hoped-for mystery," her father corrected her, laughter crinkling his eyes.

"What I mean is," Vickie went on, ignoring his interruption, "no matter what the house was used for in the past doesn't matter now. Nobody needs an Underground Railroad now."

"Sure. People can move anywhere they want to, can't they?" Diane chimed in. "Especially in our country."

Mr. Montgomery nodded agreement but said, "Well, that same kind of slavery doesn't exist in our country any longer. But that does not mean that everyone has equal opportunity. I'm afraid it is all too true that some people are more equal than others."

"What does that mean?" Diane asked, her mind grabbing for information.

"Has Vickie told you about Anna's friend whose son was arrested?" When Diane nodded, he said, "He couldn't get help because he didn't have money to hire a lawyer who would give attention to his case. I don't mean poor people can't get help. But in that case, if he had had money or his father had been an important person, he might have gotten special treatment immediately. I'm afraid our system works that way sometimes."

He kept his eyes on the road as he added thoughtfully, "And if there is injustice in our system, which I happen to believe is the best in the world, you can see that it would be true in other countries to an even greater degree. People still try to get into our country, always hoping for a better life."

He pulled the car into a parking place in front of the white stone courthouse. The girls followed him up the wide stone steps and into the cool lobby of the building. Their tennis shoes made squeaking sounds on the marble floor as they walked behind him along the wide hall. He glanced from side to side reading names and titles on the glass doors of the rooms that lined the hall.

"Ah, here we are."

He held the door for the girls to enter and then explained to a woman at a desk what they wanted. She led them down to a basement room that was like an enormous closet without windows.

She snapped on lights and gestured around at the filing cabinets and shelves along the walls. "Apparently most of the really old records were stored in here a number of years ago to make room for more current material in the main rooms. That was before I came. I don't know if anyone bothered to properly file or catalog them. We're terribly short staffed."

"Have you an approximate idea what years are in which drawers?"

"Which years are you interested in?"

45

"About the time of the Civil War."

She shook her head; her voice became brisk. "Oh, you won't find much. Very few people lived here then, I'm sure."

Mr. Montgomery smiled at her. "I know. We are interested in only one sketchy area. I've brought two expert sleuths along. If you don't mind just turning us loose, we'll see what we can find."

"You—you can't take anything away. These are valuable papers—I think."

Mr. Montgomery laughed. "We won't take anything except what we can carry by memory. I simply want to give the girls a history lesson. The best way to do that is to go to the original documents. As one who works in such a historical place, you would understand that, of course."

He smiled at her, and Vickie and Diane secretly nudged each other, trying not to laugh as they saw how she warmed under his smile and looked impressed by the business card he handed her.

When she went out and left the door open for air circulation, Mr. Montgomery gave assignments.

"Vickie, you take that section of cabinets. Just skim through the documents and look for dates. Don't bother with anything in the nineteen hundreds. Go back as far as you can in the eighteen hundreds. My recollection is that this state came into the Union in eighteen fifty-nine, but of course it was settled long before that. Diane, you do the same in that next section of drawers. Don't stop to read too much detail. And if you find docu-

46

ments or newspapers that are yellow and thin, handle them carefully. Age makes paper fragile."

After a few minutes Diane said, "There's nothing really old in these drawers."

"All right. Make your own judgment and then move on to another cabinet."

They worked in silence until Mr. Montgomery said, "Whoever stored this material here was quite careless. This drawer has documents from World War Two mixed in with material from before the First World War."

"There's stuff about the first war in this section too," Diane said. She stopped to skim through several papers and then said, "Wow, listen to this. Right at the end of the first war in—let's see—nineteen eighteen, there was a terrible flu epidemic. It tells about one place where there were nine hundred twenty-five people, and two hundred and sixty-nine died—sixty-five were kids. I didn't know you could *die* from flu."

"Dad, how about this?" Vickie broke in. She looked up from where she sat crosslegged on the floor and handed a paper up to her father.

He took it, glanced through it, and then went back to read it thoroughly, nodding his head in quick, emphatic motions, while Vickie and Diane watched him, impatient to know what it said.

When he finished reading, he explained, "This gives a brief summary of the activities of the Underground Railroad in general, not necessarily in this part of the country, though it is clear people here took some part. Apparently eighteen thirty-seven was a year when many slaves successfully

47

escaped, some through St. Louis to Chicago and farther north, eventually getting to Canada. Many people were involved in helping them. One man in Chicago was very active in the movement. He had a house with a special room that could only be reached by a trap door. He hid slaves there until he could arrange for transportation for them with someone he could trust."

He stopped to look at the girls' intent faces as they listened. "It took a great deal of courage to be a part of the Underground Railroad. People who helped slaves escape could be arrested and put in prison or heavily fined, so they didn't advertise what they were doing. According to this paper, one person suspected of being active in the movement was in this area. He lived in a small cabin so deep in the woods it was hard to find—"

"Our house?" Vickie broke in excitedly. "I mean, not *ours,* but the one we found?"

Mr. Montgomery nodded slowly. "I suppose— it *is* possible. There is only this brief reference to him. Nothing specific."

"Mr. Montgomery!" Diane's voice was breathless with eagerness. "You think there's a secret room in that kitchen, don't you? That's why you were listening to the sound it made when you knocked—you were trying to see if it was hollow-sounding!"

"Well, yes, I must admit I wondered if there could be something like that."

"But how could there be a room behind there? It would have to be cut into the side of the hill."

"Hey!" Vickie sat up straight. "A sod house!

48

Remember that story we read, Diane, about the people—what were they called? Homesteaders or something?—who sometimes dug out their house right from the ground? That's why they were called sod houses." She looked at her father eagerly.

"Hm." He stood thinking and then nodded. "Could be a similar idea. But of course the house is so remote that that itself would make it a good hiding place even without any secret room. Slaves could simply have hidden in the woods—"

"But we've read books that said they sometimes used bloodhounds to hunt the slaves' trail so they would have found them if they'd been hiding outside." Vickie banged her fist on top of a filing cabinet. "I think that's *awful!* I get mad just thinking about it."

Mr. Montgomery tapped the paper he was holding. "According to this brief mention, however he hid them, he must have been successful at it. I'm sorry that I don't know the history of that house. People—my grandfather himself—must have known it was there, even though it is so deep in the woods. Of course, it certainly has not been lived in for many years."

"Until now," Diane said.

Mr. Montgomery frowned slightly as he looked at them. "Girls, I can't deny that you saw smoke, because your mother's picture proves it was there. But it must have been from an outdoor fire by some vagrant. That is why I am warning you very seriously against wandering around alone in the woods. I want to alert the forest ranger. Someone

49

could even be deerhunting out of season. That's another reason for you to stay away. Some hunters are reckless and shoot at anything that moves."

"What could the forest ranger do if someone were in the woods?"

"Part of his job is to know who might be wandering around." He looked at his watch. "Perhaps we had better skip a library stop this time. I don't suppose it matters who owned the house originally since it has been empty for so long. And, *if* someone is there building fires—" He smiled at them as he emphasized the word. "*If* someone is there, it's someone who shouldn't be, and that is something we will leave to the forest ranger to discover. Let's stop home and let your mother know we are back from here, and then we'll make a quick trip around to see the ranger."

"We haven't had lunch yet," Vickie said as they climbed into the car. "We could get a hamburger and eat it on the way home. I saw a McDonald's a couple of blocks from here."

Her father nodded. "I'm willing to stop for a hamburger because your mother isn't expecting us home for lunch. Let's not eat in the car. We'll get quick service inside, so it won't delay us too much."

"It's funny how much better you feel after you've eaten," Diane said when they were on their way again. "I was *so* hungry."

"We noticed," Mr. Montgomery said as he looked at her in the rearview mirror and laughed. "Two hamburgers with everything and two bags of fries. And a milkshake to finish up."

"Yeah, and it doesn't show on her," Vickie grumbled.

Mr. Montgomery pulled into the gravel driveway beside the house and ran the car up even with the screened back porch. "Let's go in for a minute and let your mother know we're taking off again. She may decide to go along."

Vickie and Diane were already out of the car and clattering up the steps to the screen door. Vickie yanked, but it did not open.

"Mom! We're back."

"Is the door locked?" her father asked from behind her, his voice sounding surprised.

They heard the lock turn in the kitchen door, and Mrs. Montgomery opened it and stepped out onto the porch. One look at her face made Mr. Montgomery exclaim, "Louise! What's wrong?"

"I'm all right, but I *am* glad to see you back. I wasn't sure how long you would be away."

"How come you locked all the doors, Mom?"

"Because someone has been prowling around." She gave a shaky laugh. "In all the years we've come here, I've never felt afraid when I was here alone. But today—today I was frankly frightened."

"What happened?"

"As soon as you left, I washed a load of clothes and did a little extra cleaning since you all were out of the way. Then I went out to prune back the flowers and shrubs along the front of the house. They had gotten so straggly I was ashamed of the way they looked. Now that I think back, I believe someone was in the woods on that side of the house. I heard some rustling, but if I thought about it at all at the time, I supposed it was a squirrel—something normal and harmless."

She stopped to gesture helplessly. "I thought I locked the front door when I came in as we always do, because the door faces the road, and we are generally out here in the back. But I must not have. I changed and went for a swim and stretched out on the pier for—oh—thirty minutes, perhaps a little longer. I wasn't facing the house. And when I came back—"

She stopped and walked over to the kitchen door, gesturing inside. "Look. I left it just the way I found it."

They crowded past her into the kitchen and stood looking around at the cupboard doors standing wide with empty spaces where there had been boxes of cereal and crackers and jars of jelly and peanut butter.

"A quart of milk is gone from the refrigerator and some apples. And look in this bedroom." She pushed open the room where Vickie and Diane slept.

"Someone has been in here and left the closet door open. The clothes are shoved to one side, but there doesn't seem to be anything missing."

"Yes there is." Diane's voice came muffled from the closet. "A pair of my tennies."

"Are you sure?" Mr. Montgomery asked. "You didn't just kick them under the bed?"

"No, I had 'em right here." Then Diane leaned and picked up a pair of shoes. "Here's something funny. My new white sandals were right next to that old beat-up pair of sneakers, and they're still here. If you're going to steal something, why not steal something new?"

Mr. Montgomery put his arm around his wife. "I'm glad you were out on the pier when this happened. You might have been hurt."

"I was frightened," she admitted. "When I first stepped into the kitchen, I was afraid someone might still be in the house so I hurried over to the Sullivans. They came back with me, and that's when we saw the front door standing open. When the Sullivans left, I locked the doors and dressed. Just now you came."

"We are going to see the ranger." Mr. Montgomery's voice was grim. "Elusive smoke in the woods is one thing; housebreaking is another. Louise, please come with us. I don't like leaving you here alone."

"I'm really not afraid now, Carl. I will take my painting down by the lake—"

"I'd rather you didn't. Could you do it here on the porch? With the door locked?"

She nodded. "If it will make you feel better. But now that I've had time to think about it, I realize that whoever broke in was obviously after food. Remember when we picked up groceries Saturday? Mr. Nelson said someone had broken into the store the night before and taken food?"

"That's right. Still, that doesn't prove that was all they wanted here."

"But they only took food. My wallet was on the table with fifty dollars, and it wasn't touched. My watch was there and anyone could tell those are diamonds around the watch face. My earrings are there in plain sight—"

"Yeah, whoever it was only wanted food *and* old beat-up tennies," Diane put in.

"You go along. I'll be all right. I will lock myself in."

5

The young man in uniform who opened the door in answer to Mr. Montgomery's knock, looked at them from dark friendly eyes, a wide smile lighting his face.

"Hello! You're a welcome sight. I seldom have visitors out here in the wilds at the end of nowhere. What can I do for you?"

"We want to see what a forest ranger station looks like," Diane said impetuously. "Do you really climb up to see what's happening in the woods? How strong are the binoculars you use? And do you always wear a gun?"

"Which question do you want answered first?" he asked, his smile widening.

But Diane backed away, embarrassed, and turned to look apologetically at Mr. Montgomery. "I'm sorry. I didn't mean to barge in."

Mr. Montgomery smiled back at her and then held out his hand to the ranger. "I'm Carl Montgomery. This is my daughter Vickie and her friend Diane. We *do* want to hear your answers to Diane's questions, although we have several others to ask as well."

"I'm glad to meet you. I should introduce myself officially as a United States Forest Service fire lookout. I take it you are visiting here?"

"In a sense, yes," Mr. Montgomery answered. "However, we are regular visitors. We own property on the other side of the lake."

"Oh? Where exactly?"

"Just about directly opposite here. The Montgomery property," he added in explanation.

The ranger shook his head. "I'm sorry. The name doesn't mean anything to me. I'm newly assigned here. I've been here only a couple of months—only since May, in fact."

Mr. Montgomery nodded. "Well, then, my name would not be familiar to you. I only mention it because the property has been in my family for many years. It used to be the old family home, but now it is a summer vacation house. And sometimes I am sentimental enough to insist on dragging my family up from the city for an old-fashioned Christmas."

The ranger nodded, giving a polite smile in return, and asked, "Is there something special I can do for you? Besides answering the questions that have already been asked." He smiled at Diane as he spoke.

"Yes, there is. We wonder if you have seen smoke in the woods in the last few days?"

"Smoke?" He repeated the word, his voice cracking unexpectedly, making him seem very young. At the same time Vickie thought he straightened abruptly as he frowned back at them.

"When the girls were swimming a couple of days ago, they saw a thin column of smoke coming out of the deep part of the woods a good distance beyond our property. With the woods so dry this summer because of lack of rain, I thought I should check it out with you. Do we need to be on the alert more than usual for fire?"

"We are *always* alert." The ranger's voice was

56

defensive as he stiffened and looked back at Mr. Montgomery.

"Of course. I understand that. I was not implying inattention or carelessness on your part. But since we live here, we thought we should report what we saw."

Vickie wondered when her father was going to get around to mentioning seeing the old house and the burglary of their house and found herself bursting to blurt it out. She could feel Diane's impatience.

Then the ranger said, "I think you must be mistaken. I did not see any smoke."

He turned to the girls with his friendly smile, his voice brisk. "When the sun glares off the water, it's easy to imagine one sees things. That's particularly true this summer since we have been warning people about the unusual fire danger this season. The woods have been tinder dry. Less snow than usual last winter, I'm told, and then below normal amount of rain in the spring were contributing factors."

He talked as though he were reading a report. But he seemed more at ease as he gestured toward the door. "Would you like to look around now?"

"Sure," Vickie said, and then saw her father lean back against the wall by the window and say, "I thought at first that the girls had imagined the smoke. But then we saw it in the picture."

"The picture?" The ranger repeated the word, looking from Mr. Montgomery to the girls and back.

"Yes. My wife is an artist and was painting the

lake scene, facing in the direction from which the girls saw the smoke. She had not heard them discussing it. But when we asked later about the thin thread of smoke winding up from the trees in her picture, she assured us that she had painted the smoke in because she saw it." Mr. Montgomery paused a moment and then added in a quiet voice, "So I have no doubt the smoke *was* there."

"Oh. Well—let me see. What day did you say it was? Yesterday?"

"Sunday. Three days ago."

"Oh." The young man threw out his hands in an apologetic gesture and looked embarrassed as he cleared his throat. "Well—uh—it—it—*could* be. That you saw smoke that day, I mean." He gave an embarrassed cough. "I—uh—I—to be honest with you, I—I was not feeling well that afternoon and I—well, I must admit I did drop off to sleep a few minutes. My only comfort is that nothing happened during that time. At least I thought nothing did. But now, if you say you saw smoke—"

He stopped and shook his head, biting his lower lip. "I feel terrible to realize something could have happened while I dozed. Tell me again where you saw it, and I will certainly investigate it. I suppose it was someone building a fire to roast wieners. But any supposedly harmless fire could have disastrous consequences if not put completely out."

"But we went—" Vickie began, but was cut off by her father stepping in front of her to look at the huge map spread out along the width of one wall. He pointed. "About here, I should say. And about a mile or more in from the shore."

The ranger studied the map and shook his head. "That's very dense woods there. No trails at all that I have observed, so I don't see how anyone could have been having a picnic in there. Unless—unless someone was lost and trying to signal—a foolish thing to do, of course."

"We thought the smoke looked like a signal. But then we went and—"

Again her father interrupted. "We have something else to report, although it is nothing you are directly responsible for. It is actually a police matter. The fact is, our house was burglarized this morning. Fortunately nothing of value was taken. Whoever it was apparently was hungry, because only the kitchen cupboards were ransacked."

He stopped and then added as though the detail were not important, "Whoever it was has small feet because he—or she—also took a pair of Diane's shoes."

Vickie saw from where she stood the sudden movement of the ranger's hand as he reached behind him to grip the back of a chair, his knuckles white under the pressure.

"Well—you—you certainly must report that, of course."

Mr. Montgomery smiled as he held out his hand. "Thank you for your help Mr.—?"

"Alvarez. Robert Alvarez."

"Perhaps we will save Diane's questions and stop by another time. It must be rather a lonely job."

"Yes, and we are short staffed just now so I am doing double duty. And thanks for coming. We are always glad when citizens assist us." His smile was quick, friendly, as he opened the door and stood watching them leave.

When they were far enough from the house so that he could not hear them, Vickie asked, "How come you didn't tell him about that old house? I started to a couple of times, but you always interrupted."

"He'll probably discover it for himself," her father answered as he strode toward the car without stopping.

Vickie nudged Diane and dropped back a few steps. "Did you notice anything funny in there?"

"No. I guess I was too busy looking around. What do you mean? What kind of funny?"

"I'm not sure exactly. But I thought when Dad told about the things stolen from our house, the ranger sort of jumped."

"Maybe he thinks someone would break into his place too. After all, there's *nobody* living near him. Ask your dad if he noticed anything."

When they climbed into the car, Vickie said, "I thought he seemed kind of nervous all the time we were there. Did you, Dad?"

Mr. Montgomery nodded. "But remember, he was embarrassed to admit having gone to sleep when he was supposed to be on duty. Maybe he thought I was an inspector in disguise coming to check on him—if they do things like that in the Forest Service. Anyway, we did our duty by reporting the smoke."

"But we didn't tell about seeing the house, and I still think it and the smoke belong together somehow," Vickie insisted.

"That's too broad an assumption," her father answered. "It's clear no one has been in the house recently."

Vickie frowned, trying to hold on to the vague memory on the edge of her mind. Something in the house had told her that someone *had* been there recently. Something she had seen or sensed made her sure of it. Whatever it was, it kept slipping away without enough evidence to pin it down. Maybe if she and Diane went back alone and looked around, it would come back. If they ever got to go back alone.

When they pulled into the driveway at home, Mrs. Montgomery came out to the porch steps, holding a piece of paper.

"The office called, Carl. There have been complications in that case you have been working on for so long. They need you back for tomorrow and probably for Friday also." She looked at him sympathetically. "I had hoped you would have the entire two weeks completely away from office pressure."

He shrugged. "I had hoped so too. But if this case is moving faster than we expected, it's a good development. It has dragged on altogether too long for the good of the people involved. It has not been fair to them. Whether they are innocent or guilty is not the point. I don't like to see anyone dragged through the trauma of such long delays."

He started into the house. "This is Wednesday. I should be back Friday, but don't be alarmed if I must stay over until Saturday." He stopped, looking troubled. "The problem is that my going leaves you without a car. And with marauders around—"

Mrs. Montgomery shook her head vigorously. "I'm really not afraid, Carl. We will be careful about locking the doors. The telephone works. The refrigerator is full, even though the cupboards are a little empty. The radio and television will keep us in touch with the world. I have my paints, and the girls have the stacks of books they brought from the library. And, anyway, you will only be gone a day or two."

He frowned. "Still, I don't like it. I'll stop over at the Sullivans on the way out and ask Bill to keep watch over here."

"Hey, Dad. Maybe Francine and Pete could come back with you for over Sunday."

"Good idea," he called over his shoulder as he went into the house to change into a business suit and pack a few things in a bag.

When he came out, he stopped and looked at the girls. "Vickie. Diane. I want to repeat the warning I have already given you. I do *not* want you to go back to that house while I am away."

"Dad! Why not?"

"Couldn't we just walk over and look at it if we promise not to go in?" Diane begged.

"No, do not go near it. That is not a request, it's an order."

Mrs. Montgomery looked from him to the girls

and back again. "I've been so engrossed in my own affairs I haven't asked what you discovered about that house this morning in your research."

Mr. Montgomery looked at his watch as he said, "The girls can tell you about it. I promise that when I come back we will do some more exploring. I just do not want you doing it on your own."

The girls watched as Mrs. Montgomery walked with him to the car, their arms around each other. "One thing sure," Diane said. "Now we know your dad is more interested in that house than we thought. Don't you agree?"

Vickie nodded. "Yeah, it's not just a tree falling on us that worries him. It's because he thinks someone's hanging around there."

As she spoke, that tantalizing memory came again to whisper, *There is*.

"But your dad didn't tell us not to go back to the ranger station. We could go there tomorrow and maybe find out something about the house from him."

"Well—I don't know if we should. I think Dad really meant we should stay away from the whole thing."

"He didn't *say* so," Diane argued. "He only said not to go to the house."

"Anyway, it would be too far to walk clear around there."

"We can ride bikes. Come on, Vickie. If your dad's mad when we tell him, I'll say it was my fault. I'll take all the blame."

"That won't work with my dad. He always figures if you let someone talk you into doing something you know you shouldn't, you're just as much wrong."

"But going there wouldn't be *wrong*. If it wasn't wrong to go to the station today, why would it be tomorrow? And, anyway, your dad told the ranger we'd probably come back so we could see the station. He didn't say he'd go with us."

"Yeah, but—"

"We'll tell your mother we want to go back. Then if she says we shouldn't, we won't. OK?" Diane coaxed.

They watched Mrs. Montgomery wave him off and then turn and walk back toward them. "You see why your father has to leave the country to get away from the office, as he did in the spring. His problem is that he loses himself in each case. It's a good thing he didn't become a doctor. It would tear him apart every time a patient died."

She looked from one to the other. "Now tell me what's going on. Your father sat part of last evening staring at a sketch of something he made on his pad of legal paper and muttering, "Somehow it *must* open." Then he hunted around up in the attic, but he only came down with that old Bible."

"You heard us talking about going inside that old house and looking around."

"Yes, and your father wondered if it could have been part of the Underground Railroad. Did you find out? I was so concerned about the burglary this morning, I didn't think to ask what you discovered."

Diane broke in to explain about part of the

house being built against a hill.

"We think Dad thinks there's a secret room where slaves were hidden. He kept feeling around on the wall to find where it was. It would have to be a room built inside the hill. You know, like stories you read about pioneers who dug into the ground—"

"Of course—sod houses. Why, that idea is now very modern. I read just last week about this old/new idea of building houses underground. The pictures in the magazine were very attractive. But I can see why your father does not want you wandering around a decrepit old house. I certainly agree that it could be dangerous."

"But we do want to go back to the ranger station tomorrow and find out more about his job," Diane said.

Vickie opened her mouth to protest and then closed it again. As usual, Diane had told the truth without *really* telling it. There was more than just seeing what the ranger's job was. Still, that *was* part of the reason.

"That's a long way to walk, especially if tomorrow is as hot as today is," Mrs. Montgomery objected.

"We're planning to ride our bikes," Diane explained.

"Let me think about it during dinner. Unless—" She looked at them sharply. "Your father didn't tell you not to go back there?"

When they both shook their heads, she said, "Well, all right. If you know the way and don't stay too long."

She started up the steps to the porch, calling back, "Come rummage and see what we can agree on for dinner. Or maybe we will all end up with our own preference. And while your father is gone, we can plan something special for his birthday. If Francine and Pete do come back with him, we'll celebrate on Sunday instead of Monday. He won't mind a day-early celebration."

They set the table that was on the screened porch, so they could look out over the water that sparkled in the glow of the setting sun.

When they sat down to the chicken salad and hot biscuits, Mrs. Montgomery hesitated a moment before picking up her napkin. She slowly unfolded it and then looked at Vickie.

"I guess we should—I mean, shall—shall we pray first?"

Bowing her head, she said in her light, quick voice that trembled a little, "Thank You, God, for this food."

Vickie unexpectedly felt a lump in her throat, and she swallowed hard. It was the first time her mother had done this. Her father had started the custom of praying for the food after they came back from Israel in April. But when he was not home, they always just started eating as they had always done before the change in her father.

The awkward moment was covered by Diane's enthusiastic, "Hey, I liked that!"

As they ate, although Mrs. Montgomery asked questions about their trip to the city and to the ranger station, Vickie was sure she was thinking of something else.

"Are you worrying about us being here while Dad is gone?"

"No, not really. Perhaps I am foolish not to be concerned. But we've never had cause to feel afraid here before. I still feel whoever was here was simply hungry and not really a danger to us. Anyway, your father stopped by the Sullivans to ask them to check on us from time to time."

Vickie loved watching her mother's expressive face when she talked, and admired her clear blue eyes and thick, brushed red-gold hair. Now, staring out across the lake, her forehead creased in thought, she seemed troubled.

Meeting Vickie's eyes, she flushed and looked away. She put down her glass of iced tea and sat creasing and uncreasing her napkin. Then she said, "Honey, I want to ask you something. Have you—have you ever felt—well, as though you missed out on something because we have not raised you to—to believe in God?"

"No, not really." Vickie was as embarrassed to answer the question as she knew her mother was to ask it.

"I wondered, because—" She stopped, reached into her slacks' pocket, and pulled out a small blue leather book. "Your father was reading this this morning and left it lying face down on the table on his side of the bed. I picked it up to dust, and these words almost leaped out at me."

She looked down at the page and read in an unsteady voice: "Great is the Lord, and greatly to be praised; and His greatness is unsearchable. One generation shall praise Thy works to another, And shall declare Thy mighty acts."*

She finished reading and then said in a voice that was soft and light but at the same time troubled and unsure, "I always thought we did everything we should for you and Francine. But we never told you about God."

Vickie did not know how to answer the sad, questioning sound of her mother's voice. Then she saw Diane reach for the book. "Can I see it a minute? Is this small thing the whole Bible?"

Mrs. Montgomery shook her head. "No, it's just one book. It's called the Psalms."

Diane leafed through the pages, stopping here and there to read a few sentences. "Oh, I've heard this one before. 'The Lord is my shepherd; I shall not want.' That's pretty. I read it once in a book that had a bunch of famous poems. It goes on, 'He maketh me to lie down in green pastures: He leadeth me beside the still waters.'† It's neat to read that here by the lake, isn't it?"

Later, lying in the darkness as Diane lay asleep, thinking back over the day, Vickie's thoughts stopped at the memory of her mother's question. Her answer had been true. She had not felt cheated not knowing about God.

I've got everything I need already, her mind whispered into the quiet night.

*Psalm 145:3-4.
†Psalm 23:1-2.

6

Vickie squinted from the bright sun that reflected off the chrome handlebars of her bike as she pedaled in front of Diane. They rode along the blacktopped road that circled the deep woods surrounding the lake.

"I'm glad we don't have to go clear around the lake to get to the ranger station," she called back over her shoulder. "I haven't ridden much since we moved into the apartment last summer, so I'm not in shape for too long a ride."

"Me neither," Diane panted. "I'm in worse shape than you are. I couldn't ride all the time I had my broken leg, and then when I had the cast on for the scoliosis. It's sure a relief to have that thing off."

"Does your back hurt you ever?"

"Not much."

"Can you tell you've got that rod in your spine?"

"Nope. I don't even think about it anymore."

Diane pulled up alongside Vickie. "I'm glad this road is smooth and easy to ride on. Not much traffic, either."

Vickie glanced over at her. "How come you keep looking at me?"

"I'm not looking at you. I'm looking past you."

"Well, what for?"

"I was just wondering—"

"Well, what?" asked Vickie impatiently when Diane did not finish the sentence.

"I was just wondering how far from this road that house would be. I mean, how far into the woods?"

"I don't know."

"Your dad told the ranger it was about a mile in from the lake, so—"

"No, Diane. He said the *smoke* was about that far from the lake."

"Yeah, but it's the same thing. We know the house was where the smoke came from. It has to be, even though we can't prove it."

"You know, I've been wondering, too. What are we going to talk about to the ranger when we get there? I don't think we should even mention the house, because I just know my dad kept interrupting me on purpose yesterday every time I started to say something about it."

"But the ranger said he would go and investigate the smoke. And if he goes to the place your dad showed him on the map, then he'll see the house. He can't help it. It's there. So, now, if he says he saw where the smoke came from and we say, yeah, we did too, then—well, then he'll know we saw the house, and we can talk about it and we won't have mentioned it first."

"I suppose." Vickie slowed, trying to keep her balance as the bike wobbled. She stopped and put her feet on the ground, holding the bike steady as she thought through Diane's reasoning. She looked over toward the deep woods on their right.

"I think the house would be just about in there someplace. Way in. Maybe there used to be a path or road coming out of the woods here, but it doesn't look like it now, the way everything is grown together."

"Do you know how far it is from this road down to the lake?"

"No."

Diane stood still, looking intently into the woods. "You know what we *could* do. We could hide our bikes over there in the trees and just explore a little way in. Maybe the house is close by."

"I don't think it is."

"Why not? Look," Diane argued. "When we turn off this blacktopped road onto the gravel road that goes to your place, the gravel one isn't very long. And your house is right close to the lake."

"But see how this road has been curving. That means the woods are deeper here than they are by our house."

"We could just look a little way," Diane coaxed.

"But—"

"What?"

"Well—my dad said not to." Vickie avoided looking at Diane, not wanting to see the stubborn, closed-in look Diane's face always had when she couldn't do something she wanted to. She twisted the rubber grip on one handlebar as she said, "I think it's OK to go back to the ranger station since my dad didn't say positively not to do that."

"But we didn't actually promise in so many words that we wouldn't go back to the house. *I* didn't, anyway."

"He expects me to do what he says whether I promise in words or not."

Diane looked away, spinning one pedal around

71

and around with her foot. "Will you tell on me if I go by myself?"

Vickie shook her head. "No. But I won't cover for you, either. Not to my dad. He hates lies too much." Then, her voice stubborn, she finished, "And anyway, *I* don't think you should do it."

Diane squinted across at her then, and her eyes crinkled with laughter. "OK, you win. But somehow we've got to convince your dad that we should explore the place some more. Wouldn't it be neat if *we* found that there really is a secret place there?"

"Maybe if Francine and Pete come with my dad, they'll go with us. I know Pete would." She wiped her sweaty hands on her shorts. "We'd better ride faster or we'll never get there."

They were red-faced and sweaty when they finally turned off the blacktopped road onto the circular graveled drive that led to the ranger station. They bumped over the gravel to the red brick building set neatly in a closely trimmed grassy area. A row of petunias bordered the driveway and massed in a splurge of color on each side of the white door.

They parked their bikes, kicking down the stands, and knocked on the closed door. When there was no answer, they knocked again, harder.

"He must be out checking for fires."

"Maybe he's gone looking for that smoke," Diane exclaimed. With regret in her voice she added, "If we'd come sooner, maybe we could have gone with him. That would be a perfect way to get back to the house without disobeying your father."

"Try knocking again. Maybe this is a sound-proof door."

"Or maybe he's taking another nap." Diane laughed, but stopped quickly when the door opened.

"Hello." The ranger looked at them. "You're alone this time."

"Yeah. We hope we're not bothering you. We didn't get a chance to look around here yesterday, and we got to wondering if you found out anything about the smoke, so we decided to ride our bikes over and ask." Diane's eager face looked up at him as she rushed the words out without stopping for breath.

The young ranger lounged in the doorway, leaning against the door frame with his arms folded. He smiled down at them.

"You are on your way to being good citizens. I appreciate your notifying me about what could have developed into something serious."

"Did you see anything?"

"No. I'm glad to tell you that I checked it out and there's no evidence of a fire."

"You went over there?" Diane asked eagerly.

"Yes. That is, as near as I could figure out the spot from what your father said."

"But did you see the——"

Diane stopped when Vickie moved suddenly, bumping her arm, and saying quickly, "Could we come in and look at what you do? We didn't get a chance to see much yesterday."

He shifted his position slightly to stretch one arm out against the opposite door frame, not moving out of the way. "Tell you what. I'm glad to have company. I've discovered that I'm not all that exciting a person to be with all the time." He grinned and gave such an exaggerated shrug of his shoulders that they couldn't help smiling back at him.

"The most interesting part of my job is outside the station instead of inside." He gestured with his head toward the room behind him. "This is where I make out reports, and that's pretty dull stuff. Wait here a minute until I get a pair of strong field glasses, and I'll show you my outside routine."

As he shifted to turn back into the room, Vickie took a step forward, trying to peer past him. He turned toward her, again blocking the doorway.

"I suggest that you wheel your bikes out of the hot sun so you don't blister your legs when you ride home. While you do that, I'll get the glasses and be right with you."

He watched them walk to their bikes before turning back into the room, partly closing the door.

"You didn't let me ask about the house," Diane sputtered.

"I thought we agreed we wouldn't. Anyway, didn't you think it was funny the way he just stood right in the doorway and didn't let us in?"

"Well, I guess. But I was so busy trying to figure out how to find out more about the house—"

"I was suspicious," Vickie interrupted, "and I was sure he was purposely keeping us out. I could see a door across the room that was open just a tiny crack. Just as you started asking if he had seen the house, I saw the door close."

"You mean someone else is in there?"

"Shh, here he comes."

The ranger crossed the driveway, his face and manner relaxed and friendly. "You'll have to tell me something about yourselves. Do you remember my name—Robert Alvarez? I think I told you yesterday that I've only been here since May. I came from California."

"Are you all alone here?"

He smiled at Diane. "If you're asking if I'm married, the answer is no. Maybe that's why I'm lonely. But that will change soon, since I am engaged to a girl who graduated from college with me." He looked at them. "But now tell me about yourselves. You're not sisters, I know."

"I'm Vickie Montgomery and she's Diane Stewart, and we're best friends. But we really do want to know what you do here all the time."

"OK, Vickie and Diane. I can tell you that a ranger's job, in a place as heavily wooded as this, is very important. Especially at times when everything is so dry. A fire has terrible power to destroy."

"My dad told us about one that happened here a long time ago. He said people tried to hide in ditches hoping the fire would skip over them, but some of them burned to death anyway. And one old couple climbed down a ladder into a well to escape the fire. But when neighbors came to look for them, they had drowned."

"Even the cows' feet were burned from running on the hot ground," Diane said. "People lost their houses and barns and everything."

The ranger nodded, his face sober. "You know, even lightning can start a fire sometimes. So, while rain is welcome, occasionally the lightning that accompanies a storm can be dangerous."

He led the way up the steep steps to the lookout platform and handed Vickie the field glasses. "Here. Try looking through these. You'll have to focus to suit your eyes. But then you'll see how clearly everything shows up."

Vickie looked, sweeping the glasses slowly around the curving rim of the lake. "There's our house, but I can't see my mother."

"Let me see." Diane took the glasses and looked in the direction Vickie pointed. Then she swept them around the lake, and Vickie knew she was trying to locate the hidden house. After a moment she handed the glasses back to Vickie, her eyes saying, "See if you can find it."

She studied the woods carefully, trying to estimate the distance from their house to where they had struck off into the woods. But though the glasses brought details into clear focus, the old house was apparently too deep among the trees to show up.

As she moved the glasses back and forth, trying to pinpoint the exact spot, she heard the ranger's amused voice. "Are you looking for a special place?"

"Well—just—just looking." She knew Diane was dying to ask about the house, impatient as she was with the order not to.

The ranger took the glasses then and swept them in a steady arc around the lake. Watching him carefully, Vickie asked, "Did you walk *clear* over to where we saw the smoke?"

"Uh—what? Oh. Yes, in that general direction. Though as I said, your father was not precise in what he said about the location. And, of course, distances are deceptive in the woods when you are going through them on the ground."

"Well, it was right over *there!*" Diane pointed as she spoke, her voice so positive that she sounded angry.

He focused through the glasses again and then said, "If you're so sure, I'll check there more carefully and let you know if I find anything. How's that?"

"We could meet you there if you let us know when you're going," Diane said eagerly.

He thought for a moment and then shook his head. "Thanks, but that would be a pretty long walk for you in the hot sun—"

"We wouldn't mind," Diane interrupted. "We would just walk along the lake and then cut through the woods like we did the other time."

"You walked that far? You might have gotten lost. Don't do it again." His voice was sharp and he looked at them both sternly.

"Oh, we've done it twice. The first time by ourselves, and then the next time my father went with us, and we went inside the house."

The words were out before Vickie even knew she was going to say them. She could have kicked herself. After keeping Diane from telling, she had gone and blurted it out.

But she was not prepared for his startled reaction as he repeated, "A house? Out there in the middle of the forest?"

"Yes," Diane answered. "It's a big old house all by itself. If you were over where we said, you would have seen it."

"I must not have gone quite far enough." He flashed his friendly grin then, his teeth white against his tanned skin. "Well, then, that would naturally explain the smoke. That's what chimneys in houses are for. I was afraid we were talking about a careless smoker or camper who can be more dangerous in the woods than a wild animal."

Now that they had said this much, Vickie knew there was no point in keeping back more information. She listened as Diane said, "But that doesn't explain the smoke at all, because no one lives there. Even Vickie's father said that. You see, it's a real old place. I mean *really* old."

That flicker of something about the house moved in Vickie's mind again, a memory of something that had not fit the blank, empty appearance. The memory slipped away as the ranger said briskly, "I promise you that I will double check this. Unfortunately, I am so new here that I am not yet familiar with all the places danger might lurk. And an old, unlived-in house can be a source of danger."

"Couldn't we please go with you when you check it out?" Diane begged.

The ranger led the way down to the ground, his voice full of regret as he answered, "Since I would be on official business, no. I'm sorry. Let me see about it first, since that's my job. And let me warn you to be careful about wandering around by yourselves."

He looked at them, his face and voice serious. "After all, your own house was broken into. Have you discovered who that was?"

Vickie shook her head. "But I'm sure my dad reported it to the police."

He walked with them to their bikes and watched them wheel out from the shade of the trees. "How long are you staying at the lake?"

"Another week at least. It depends on whether my dad can stay the whole time. There's a big trial coming up soon, and he may have to go back for it."

The ranger turned abruptly. "A trial? Your father is a lawyer?" His tone was sharp.

Vickie nodded as she stood by her bike, looking over at his house. If only they could get back inside. It really was not any of their business if someone was visiting him. But he had not wanted to let them in, and that door *had* closed.

Then she heard Diane exclaim, "I'm so *thirsty!* Could we have a drink of water before we start back? The sun is murder when you're riding a bike such a long way."

"Of course. Come in."

They followed behind him on their bikes with Vickie mouthing to Diane, "Great idea."

He held the door open for them to enter. Vickie watched closely as he pulled open a cupboard and got down glasses. He did not act as though he were trying to hide anything from them or make a loud noise to warn somebody that they were there.

They each drank a glass of water slowly, looking around. Vickie tried not to stare at the closed door across the room.

The ranger pointed out the tiny kitchen space. "I'm a pretty good cook," he said with a laugh. "I don't do anything fancy, but I can make pretty good chili."

Then he crossed the room and threw open the door to a small room, gesturing at the narrow bed and the easy chair beside an end table with a lamp.

"They fix us up pretty comfortably here. The closet will have to be enlarged before I'm married, or my wife and I will argue over who gets to use it."

"Do all forest rangers live all the time in a small house like this?" Vickie tried to sound politely interested even though she really was not, because she could not get her mind off all the other questions that seemed to have no answers.

"Oh, no. Living situations vary depending on what kind of a job you have in the Forest Service, and also where you are. I'm hoping eventually to work for the Park Service in one of the National Parks as a tourist guide. Right now I'm interested in the Great Smoky Mountains National Park in Tennessee."

"Hey!" Diane turned eagerly. "My grandmother gave me a subscription to *National Geographic* for a Christmas present, and one of 'em has a whole bunch of articles about National

Parks. When I go home, I'm going to get it out and read it again."

"Maybe some day you'll come down on vacation, and I'll show you around." He smiled at them. "Any other questions before I get back to work?"

"No, we'd better be going," Vickie answered reluctantly.

He followed them out into the heat, lifting his hand in a wave as they started off. "Take it easy. Don't ride too fast," he called after them.

When they turned onto the blacktopped road, they looked back and saw him still watching them.

Diane waved at him again. "I like him!"

"I do, too. But remember, he didn't tell us the truth. I don't think he went and looked for that smoke at all. But why did he pretend he had?"

"I guess maybe he thought we were just a couple of nosy kids." Diane scowled as she always did when she was bothered by something. "Another thing—he did purposely show us that that room was empty. Didn't you think?"

"Yes. And I think that proves someone was there. One thing I know. I *saw* that door close. And it did not close all by itself!"

7

"Somehow we've *got* to get back into that house," Diane burst out as they rode home.

"Yeah, but we can't till my dad gets back tomorrow or Saturday."

"Maybe your mother would go with us," Diane suggested hopefully.

"Uh-uh." Vickie shook her head. "I don't think we should even ask her, because my dad said—"

"I know. I know! We're not supposed to go."

Diane's voice was sharp with impatience, and Vickie snapped back, "It's not my fault. I want to go as much as you do, but I have to do what my dad says. So don't blame me!"

"I'm not. It's just that—well, it's silly not to be able to do a simple thing like walking over and looking at the place. Just looking. Especially since we've already been there. It'd be different if we didn't know the way."

"I guess my dad has a good reason."

Vickie kept her eyes straight ahead, her jaw clenched, and her back stiff as they rode the rest of the way home in angry silence. They parked their bikes at the end of the driveway and walked around the side of the house to the back door. At the sound of their footsteps, a dog got up from where it lay at the foot of the steps and barked loudly.

"Bowser!" Vickie exclaimed. "That's all right, boy. We belong here."

Mrs. Montgomery looked around from where

she sat at her easel and called through the screened window. "It's about time you were home. I was about to send Bowser out to look for you. Mrs. Sullivan brought him over, apologizing that they didn't think of loaning him to us last night. They said they would feel safer about us if he were here, though she said he is too friendly to be much of a watchdog."

The girls patted the dog, carefully not looking at each other, and started up the steps to the screen door.

"Wait a minute. The door's locked." Mrs. Montgomery unhooked the screen. "Remember, we promised your father we wouldn't take any unnecessary chances."

"See?" Vickie muttered, her glance at Diane cold. "Even my mother does what she's supposed to."

Diane did not answer as she stalked into the house, her thin shoulders rigid, her head held high. It was a miserable evening. After supper they played games with Mrs. Montgomery, who looked from one to the other, but did not ask questions. The day's riding had tired them, so they went to sleep quickly, the cold, unfriendly silence a barrier between them.

Vickie woke up first the next morning and sneaked out to dress in the bathroom. Her mother was sitting on the porch enjoying a cup of coffee. The warm sun was slanting through the trees and reflecting off the silver coffeepot on the table.

"The birds sound much happier than you look this morning." Mrs. Montgomery pushed a bowl

83

of cold cereal, strawberries, and the squat blue jug of milk across the table. "You girls still not speaking?"

"She's so stubborn!" Vickie chomped morosely on a mouthful of crisp cereal.

"That's one reason she is such a good friend."

Vickie stirred the cereal in the bottom of the bowl, not looking at her mother. "Don't know what you mean."

"Well, for one thing, it makes her stick with you in spite of *your* stubbornness." Mrs. Montgomery's tone was light as she smiled across at Vickie's glum face.

Vickie looked at her and then quickly looked away. After a minute, she smiled faintly in return. "I guess. But this time—" She stopped, not wanting to tell what the argument was about.

"Considering Diane's past, I think she had to develop a stubborn streak in order to survive. Don't you?"

Vickie spread butter and jam on a piece of toast, remembering the one time Diane had given a glimpse of the fights she had heard between her parents when she was little. She had begun then to build a wall around herself for protection. Now the wall kept out the hurt of her father's desertion and the hurt of the bitterness that made her mother drink. Naturally Diane would not understand the reason for her parents' rules. To Diane they meant, "You can't have fun," instead of, "This is for your protection because we care about you."

She heard her mother's warm voice. "Vickie, true friendship doesn't shift back and forth depending on feelings and circumstances. It always wants the best for the other person. Try to be a dependable friend, honey, someone Diane can always count on for understanding and help. I'm afraid she doesn't get that understanding at home."

She stood up then as the phone rang, and Vickie listened to her end of the conversation while she thought about Diane.

"Good morning, Mrs. Sullivan . . . No, everything was quiet . . . I will be happy to keep Bowser until Carl returns if you insist . . . Yes, he barked a few times in the night just to let us know he was still taking care of us . . . Yes, we're keeping the doors locked . . . Thank you for calling."

She hung up the phone and turned as Diane came from the bedroom. "Good morning! I hope you girls can find something to keep you occupied today. I am going to concentrate on finishing your father's picture, because he might possibly get home this evening. I want it ready for his birthday. But I'm also going to bake a blueberry pie for the Sullivans to thank them for letting us borrow Bowser. Did you hear him last night?"

Diane shook her head, pouring a bowl of cereal and not looking at Vickie. Then, when Mrs. Montgomery went into the kitchen, Diane mumbled, "I'm sorry I was so bratty last night."

"That's OK. I guess I was, too. Let's go swim as soon as we can after breakfast."

The swim made them hungry for an early lunch. When they finished, Mrs. Montgomery said, "Before you find something more interesting to do,

85

please run this pie over to the Sullivans for me. Oh, and take the dog with you. He's more of a bother than a help in the daytime. I can't concentrate when he whines at the screen door."

Bowser bounded along, stopping to sniff the ground and make quick scurrying detours. "That's one thing I hate about apartment living, that we're not allowed to have a dog."

"Yeah, me too," Diane said. "But my mother wouldn't have one anyway. She thinks a dog's too much bother."

Mrs. Sullivan was weeding a flower bed and stood up with a welcoming smile. "Well, thanks so much!" She took the pie and then stooped to pet Bowser. "I'm glad he has some young company for a few days. I'm afraid he gets pretty tired of two old folks like us. He's always begging us to go for a walk—the way he's doing now with his tail wagging so furiously. But we've gotten lazy, and Bill ends up just throwing a stick for him to chase."

"*We'll* take him for a walk," Diane offered, her face alight with eagerness. "We don't have anything else special to do."

"Fine. You can be sure he won't get lost. He has been here so many summers that the woods are a second home to him. Vickie, when do you expect your father back?"

"Tomorrow for sure. Maybe tonight."

"That's good. We've been on the lookout for anyone prowling around, but haven't seen anyone. Have a good walk, and keep Bowser as long as you need him," she called after them.

"Let's walk along the lake," Diane suggested. "Maybe if we throw sticks in the water, he'll bring 'em back."

Bowser raced after the sticks, plunging into the cold lake and coming back to shake water over them vigorously. He chased squirrels and sniffed under and around every fallen log they passed. There was still a strained feeling between them, and Vickie was glad the dog was along to give them something to talk about and laugh at.

Suddenly Diane stopped. "Here we are, Vickie. Here's the first signal we tied on the trees." The expression on her face was defiant as she went on, "I'm going over to the house. Maybe you'll say I shouldn't, but I'm going anyway. Your father can bawl me out all he wants to when he gets back. That is, if you tell on me. And you probably will."

She looked at Vickie and then turned and started walking slowly into the woods. Vickie watched her thin figure in the red and white striped shirt and white shorts as she stopped to straighten one of the red strips of torn scarf and then retie it higher on the tree trunk. She looked back over her shoulder. "Coming?"

Vickie looked down at Bowser as he rooted under a fallen log and then with short, excited barks dashed from Vickie to Diane and back to Vickie. After all, Dad had been mostly worried about their going to the house alone in case something happened to them. But if they had Bowser with them, they really wouldn't be alone. A dog was always a protection. He could bark and scare anybody off. And, if anything happened and they needed help, they could send him back for help. Mother could get the Sullivans to come with her. Besides, they would not stay long.

She looked at Diane moving slowly away, still looking back over her shoulder with the questioning look on her face. She took a step in that direction as she had another reassuring thought. The ranger might be there, so they would not be alone. Their being alone was *really* the reason Dad had told them not to go.

She whistled at Bowser. "Come on, boy." Then she called, "Wait up, Diane."

"Don't come unless you want to," Diane warned. "Don't come just for me, because I'm going whether you do or not."

"I'm coming because we've got Bowser with us," Vickie answered, squashing the uneasy feeling inside that warned, *Don't do it.* "With Bowser along we won't be alone, and that's what my dad was worried about."

Diane turned then and walked ahead, checking the trees for the ragged strips of red cloth, while Vickie kept Bowser near by calling his name and whistling to him.

It did not seem to take as long to get to the house this time. They came upon it suddenly and stopped at the fringe of trees by the clearing to look at its emptiness. Bowser bounded across the cleared space, tangling himself in the weeds, and sending a squirrel chattering up a tree.

"Wanna go in?"

"That's why we came," Vickie retorted. "As

long as we've already done what we're not supposed to, there's no point in stopping now."

They walked slowly across the clearing and up the three worn steps to the porch. The front door creaked as they pushed it open and stood in the doorway.

"Wait a minute," Vickie said. "I'm going to get that big stick over there in the yard to prop the door open. That way it will be lighter in here."

She did not say aloud her real reason: with the door open, they could get out faster if they had to.

Diane stood in the middle of the living room, looking around. "I'd sure like to see what this place looked like after Anna got through with it. Bet it would look real nice."

"I don't know if even Anna could get rid of all this dirt." Vickie rubbed her bare arms in the closed-in chill of the grimy room as she glanced nervously around. She jumped at Bowser's sudden lunge at something that scurried across the floor. "What was that?"

"A mouse, I think. Come on, Vickie. We don't want to stay very long. Let's just go look in the kitchen for a couple of minutes and see if we can find the secret place your dad was looking for. If we could find it and prove that this house really was a part of the Underground Railroad, it would make such a neat report for school. We could even write a story about it for the school paper."

"Wait!" Vickie grabbed Diane's arm and pulled her back. "Did you hear that noise? It sounded as though it came from out there—from the kitchen."

"I didn't hear anything. Bowser's making so much racket. What did it sound like?"

"I don't know. Like something falling."

Diane hesitated. "Well, let's—let's take Bowser and just push the door open real slowly and peek in."

"O-OK. Here, boy!"

But the dog's excitement took him out the front door and down the porch steps after another mouse that escaped his reaching paws.

"Now what, Diane?"

"Let's just take a quick look. Bowser's right out front. We'll yell for him if we have to."

Vickie walked close on Diane's heels, looking back over her shoulder. "It sure feels like eyes staring at us." She whispered, but her voice sounded loud in the emptiness.

"Must be all the people who used to live here." Diane tried to laugh, but she did not sound very confident. She cautiously pushed open the kitchen door and looked in. Then she clutched Vickie's hand and whispered, "Look!"

"Wh—what?"

"There it is! There's the door your dad was trying to find!"

She started across the room to a low door that stood slightly open in the opposite wall, but Vickie grabbed her back.

"Wait, Diane! It wasn't like that the other day. That means someone's been here. Maybe someone's still here. Maybe that's the noise I heard. Let's go!"

Diane stopped, and they listened to the silence. "I hate to go when we're so close to discovering the secret," she whispered.

"We can come back tomorrow with my dad. Now that we know it's there, he can find it again," Vickie whispered back.

The girls stood close together, looking and listening. The door opening off the kitchen to the bedroom looked just as it had the other day. The dirty table was bare; the chairs stood just as they had. There was nothing to show that anyone had been there. Nothing but the mysterious hiding place now standing open.

"Vickie—I bet the ranger was here," Diane said, her voice sounding braver.

"Then why didn't he say so? That makes it worse if he purposely is fooling us about not knowing this house is here."

"Vickie, let's just peek in a minute to see what it looks like in there, and then we'll go."

They tiptoed across the room and stooped to peer through the narrow opening into the dim interior of what looked like a closet.

"Look!" Diane's excitement made her stammer. "I-It's a-about the size of that pantry in your mother's k-kitchen. It *has* to be the place that man hid the slaves. Can you figure out how it opens? I still don't see any doorknob or handle. Isn't this neat? Wait'll we tell your dad!"

"OK, but come on, let's go. We've seen it."

"Let's just pull the door a little wider open, OK?" Diane begged. "If we can just get a better idea of what it really looks like in there. But it's kind of dark. Wish we'd thought to bring a flashlight—"

"That's what we can do tomorrow. Come *on*, Diane!"

"Come on, Vickie, help me pull. Please? Just so we can see in a little better."

The door scraped a little on the floor as they tugged it open with Diane leaning to look in.

"I'm just going to step inside a minute."

"Diane, wait!"

But she squeezed through the opening into the small room. "It's sure dirty and smelly in here. But look, Vickie." Her voice rose with excitement. "I think this really is the hill in here. I mean the room is dug into the hill, but it's not just dirt all around. It's sort of like a panelled room. It's got wood on the sides—boards sort of—and on the floor too. Come in and look. It's too hard to describe."

Vickie ducked her head to keep from hitting the top of the doorway and stepped inside. She straightened up and looked around though it was too dim to see clearly. Something brushed her face and she jumped back, reaching her hands to rub her face. Then she felt the same soft brushing on her bare arms.

"Diane, something's on me!"

"Where?"

"All over. I'm going out."

"It's probably just cobwebs. They're all over me too. They feel terrible, but at least they won't bite."

"I bet there are things in here that do. If we saw mice out in the rest of the house, I bet they're here too. Maybe even rats."

"I wish we could see better——"

"Well, we can tomorrow. I know my dad will come back with us even though he won't like it that we came today." Vickie shivered as she looked around, feeling the silence. "It must have been horrible to be in here, hiding from someone. I wouldn't get closed in here for anything——"

She stopped abruptly at a scraping sound behind her and whirled in time to see the light from the kitchen disappear as the door slammed shut.

Diane lunged past her. "Vickie, push on it!"

But they were too late. The door would not budge.

8

They yelled and pounded on the wood and then leaned back against the side of the small room, panting from the exertion and from fright.

"What made it go shut?" Vickie's voice was sharp with fear.

"I—I don't know."

The quaver in Diane's voice made Vickie furious. "I knew there was someone in the house! I *told* you I felt eyes staring at us."

"But we didn't see anybody."

"Well, somebody shut the door!" Vickie snapped back.

In the silence the faint, far-off sound of barking made them realize how soundproof the room was. Bowser's bark sounded miles away.

"He'll—he'll go home, and my mother will wonder where we are and come looking," Vickie said, trying to keep her voice steady.

"The Sullivans said he'd never get lost in the woods, so that means he'll go back."

They turned toward each other in the darkness, and then Vickie voiced the question she knew was in Diane's mind. "But how do we know he's smart enough to let them know where we are?"

Instead of answering, Diane said, "Vickie, I'm sorry! This is all my fault. If I hadn't wanted my way, we wouldn't be in this mess. I knew it was wrong to come, and I got you into it as well as myself."

Vickie shook her head. "I can't blame you. I

94

talked myself into coming because I wanted to. You're not to blame for what I purposely did."

Diane pushed on the wall again, running her fingers up and down where she thought the edge of the door was. "It's no use. There's no way to open it from the inside. If this really was fixed to hide slaves by someone who could be put in prison if they were discovered, then he fixed it so they wouldn't be discovered. We're kidding ourselves if we think we can get out by ourselves."

Vickie's voice came small and scared. "I saw a TV program once where people were trapped in a little place, and—and—after a while they used up all the air."

But Diane said quickly, "I still say if this was built to keep people safe, the man thought of that. He must have fixed it so there'd be enough air."

"But that would have been years and years ago. Maybe air holes or whatever he made got filled up with dirt—"

"Vickie! Don't imagine all sorts of stuff! It's bad enough as it is!"

They sat down on the floor against the wall, hugging their knees against the chill of the room. "It's funny, it's so hot outside and so cool in here," Diane said.

"I guess it's because we're sort of inside the hill." Then Vickie burst out, "I wish I'd never heard of the Underground Railroad!"

She leaned her head against the rough wood of the wall and closed her eyes to shut out the darkness and the hopelessness of their surroundings.

But she could not shut out her frightened thoughts. A question kept asking itself, *Who shut the door?* It could not possibly have shut accidentally. They both had pulled hard to get it open far enough for them to squeeze through. Whoever had discovered the secret door had left it open. And was in the house when they got there. And then had shut the door on them, trapping them. If only they had not come back!

As she sat in the scary silence of the dark room, memory suddenly clicked into place the reason she had known this was not an empty house.

"Diane," she said, not opening her eyes.

"What?" Diane's voice was now sounding small and scared.

"When we were here before and my dad was having us pretend to be detectives, I picked up one of those plates and a fork. There were bits of food sticking to the plate. Dried food, but not old food. Someone had used the plate recently. I'm sure of it."

"There's another thing, Vickie, that I've been sitting here remembering. When we looked in that bedroom, everything was old and dirty. But not the blankets. They looked new. And clean."

Diane jumped up and began pounding on the wall. "There must be something we can do to get out of here. Let's push again and yell."

But Vickie grabbed Diane's arm. "Wait! If someone shut us in on purpose, as long as we're in here, we're safe from whoever is out there."

"I don't feel safe, but maybe you're right."

"We just have to wait till my dad comes looking

for us." Vickie tried to see the luminous dial on her watch. "Can you believe we've only been here a half hour! We'll have to stay here all the rest of the day."

"Or all night if your dad doesn't come home until tomorrow."

"Then my mother will come. When Bowser goes home without us, she'll get worried."

"But if he isn't smart enough to lead her here, will she think about the house? She knows your dad said we weren't supposed to come back here. Maybe she'll just think we're lost in the woods."

"I think she'll go to the forest ranger and ask him to help."

"But what if—what if he's the one who shut us in here?"

Vickie had already thought of that, but did not want to say so. She tried to sound brave even though she did not feel like it. "Well, if we have to wait until tomorrow, it won't kill us. We'll get hungry, but we won't starve in one day. I know my dad will come as soon as he gets back. The only thing is—" She stopped, feeling miserable. "I hate to face him."

"Me too. But it will be worth it to get out of here."

"It serves us right if we have to stay all night."

"All this happened just because I insisted on doing what I wanted to." Vickie knew from the sound of Diane's voice that she was fighting back tears.

"There's only one thing," Vickie said hesitantly.

"What?"

97

"I just hope my dad comes before whoever shut us in here decides to come back."

"Oh, Vickie!" Diane reached to grab her hand. "I'm really getting scared!"

Vickie nodded silently, not wanting to put into words her own fright. Then in the cold darkness she heard Diane's voice.

" 'Though I walk through the valley of the shadow of death, I will fear no evil, for thou art with me.' Do you think that's true, Vickie? That was part of the poem I read in your dad's book. Does that mean God is here? With us?"

Vickie rubbed her arms, feeling the cold of the ground surrounding them. But she felt cold also because of Diane's question. For God to be there did not seem to her like a comforting thought. You usually did not think of God unless you were going to die. And anyway, did God get you out of a mess you deliberately got yourself into? All she could answer was a whispered, "I don't know."

They sat close together in the dark, their backs against the wall, their legs pulled up tight against them with their arms hugging their knees. Vickie could feel Diane's thin figure shivering in the damp chill of the underground room, and moved closer to her for body warmth.

"I wish I'd worn jeans instead of shorts," Diane said, her teeth chattering. "I get cold so easily."

The minutes dragged by as they sat huddled together. Vickie strained to see her watch, afraid it had stopped, and held it to her ear for the reassuring tick-tick-tick. The darkness seemed to shut them in from the world. She shifted her cramped position and felt something on her neck. "Ooh!" She shrank away from the wall.

"What is it?" Diane started up.

"Just another cobweb, I guess, but it felt like a bug." She rubbed her cold arms, feeling the goose-bumps. "Maybe we should be glad it's too dark to see what's in here."

"It must have been awful for them," Diane said suddenly. "Think what it must have been like to be hunted like animals and have to hide in a place like this. And for no reason except that you had black skin."

"When I've read in social studies about slaves trying to escape, it was just words to me. I never thought about how they *felt*."

"Think how scared they must have been. Especially if there were dogs chasing them. They'd have to keep their babies from crying and giving away where they were hiding. That must have been awful hard if the babies were sick or hungry."

"I suppose—sometimes—there were girls our age hiding here." Vickie's voice was somber, and she shivered. "I've never thought how lucky we are to be born the way we were, with our life so easy."

"Even me. I've sometimes thought I had it hard—" Diane broke off, the sentence unfinished.

They sat in silence, thinking of those long-ago figures who had huddled in stark fear in this narrow, dark space, listening for harsh demanding voices and the growl of dogs.

"Your dad *will* come?"

Diane's voice was a question, and Vickie answered quickly, "Of course he will!"

"He won't know where we are."

"He'll guess right away that we came here——"

"I mean, he won't know where we are *here*. He won't know how to open the door. He didn't yesterday."

"He'll figure it out somehow. He'll have more reason to hunt for it in order to find us. And we'll yell when we're sure it's my dad out there."

"Shh." Diane clutched Vickie's arm. "Did you hear that? Weren't those voices?"

"No, but let's yell. I don't care if it is someone dangerous. If the door opens, we'll run like crazy."

They pounded and shouted. "Help! We're in here! There's a door! Find how it opens!"

Finally they leaned back against the wall, panting from the effort. Vickie rubbed her bruised knuckles. "I'm sure it's too early for it to be my dad. I just thought maybe Bowser had brought my mother and the Sullivans. I'm sure she'd get them to help find us."

"I didn't hear any barking, so it couldn't have been Bowser. Maybe he never even went back. He may still be fooling around in the woods. Or maybe he went back to the Sullivans, and they didn't send him back to your place right away." Diane slumped against the wall.

"I keep telling myself it's better not to yell for help until we're sure it's my dad coming. Then I think I don't care who opens the door as long as we can get out of here. I feel as though the walls are shrinking in on us."

"What time is it now?"

Vickie peered at her watch. "I can't tell for sure. I think it's stopped. You may be right about the time. Maybe we haven't been in here as long as it seems."

"If your dad gets back late, and it's too dark to see to come here, he'll have to wait until morning."

"Diane, there's one thing I know. He'll come. He'll figure out something. He won't go to bed until we're home safe."

She knew what she said was true, but in spite of it, panic rose at the thought of spending hours more, perhaps a cold dark night, in this narrow place with an even deeper darkness outside closing around them.

Then in the silence she heard Diane's voice, scratched and forlorn. "You're lucky. You can always count on your folks."

Vickie reached again for Diane's hand as they sat side by side, leaning against the wall. Even though they were both helpless, the touch of someone else was comforting.

Diane's laugh was weak and trembling as she said, "It's funny, but I keep seeing those words in your dad's book. 'Though I walk through the valley of the shadow of death, I will fear no evil, for thou art with me.' I've been sitting here saying them over and over in my mind without really thinking about what they mean. I guess they're sort of like a charm to keep danger away."

Vickie wondered again. *Does God take care of you when you are to blame for the mess you're in?*

She heard Diane echo the thought as she said, "I guess I shouldn't expect help from your father when I just went ahead and did what he said not to. Or help from God either," she added in a strained, self-conscious voice.

She did not seem to expect an answer, and Vickie was glad, because she did not know what to answer.

Then Diane gave a small laugh. "If my mother heard me talking about God, she'd really blow up. She thinks religion is for dummies. If she knew that I—that I—" She broke off the sentence, tightening her hold on Vickie's hand.

Vickie sat thinking about it. Dad was no dummy, and yet he found it necessary to believe in God. And it certainly had made him happier.

Diane jerked, twisting sideways, and exclaimed, "Oh, Vickie! Something ran over my foot!"

They both jumped to their feet, and Vickie said, "It was probably a mouse. I hope that's all it was. No telling what else is in here."

"You think maybe—snakes?"

"I don't know. Diane, let's yell again!"

They pounded and called until finally Vickie leaned against the wall. "It's no use. I don't think my folks will be able to hear us."

"Just because no one answers now, doesn't mean they don't hear us. It means no one is out there to hear."

"Or else it means that whoever shut the door doesn't want to open it." Just saying the words made the unknown enemy seem so real and close that Vickie had to bite her lip and blink hard to keep back frightened tears.

"I'm so tired," Diane said, her voice small and empty. "But I'm scared to sit down again in case something else runs over me. I used to think it was silly that girls were always supposed to be afraid of things like mice and bugs. I never thought I got scared easily. But I am now."

"It's because it's dark in here," Vickie answered. "Things always seem worse in the dark."

"Especially this kind of dark." Vickie could tell that Diane was looking around from the way her voice sounded. "It's not a nice soft dark like when you're in bed and it's quiet and the stars are shining. This dark seems so threatening. And the worst thing is that maybe this dark place is safer than what's on the other side of the door."

"And I'm hungry, too. I wish I'd put a couple of chocolate bars in my pocket." Vickie sighed. "I was going to after lunch, but I was afraid they would melt all over my shorts."

"Well, just think. This way you'll lose a couple more pounds." Diane tried for a laugh and ended coughing and choking.

"The trouble is, you'll lose too, and you shouldn't." Vickie gave a long, tired sigh. "What time do you think it was when we got here?"

"It was eleven o'clock when we got back from swimming, and we ate lunch right away. Then we went to the Sullivans with the pie. And then it took us about—how long, do you think to walk here?"

"I don't know. A couple of hours maybe? Bowser kept fooling around."

"OK, say we got here by two o'clock," Diane said. "And say we've been here a couple of hours at least."

"Oh, yeah, at least. More like four or five."

"Well, it probably *seems* longer than it really is." Talking seemed to take away some of Diane's fright. "It may not be any later than five o'clock. And even if it's as late as seven o'clock, it would still be light outside."

"And if that's what time it is, my mother is going nuts wondering where we are. She'll maybe think whoever broke into our house has got us trapped someplace, and she'll call the police. At least she'll call the forest ranger. She won't know enough to suspect him."

"Vickie, do you really think maybe he's the one who shut us in here? He seemed so nice. I really liked him."

"I don't know. Everything is so mixed up now. It's even funny to think that it's hot and light outside when it's so dark and cold in here."

"Let's do something to pass the time," Diane suggested.

"We could count the way my dad said a person can figure out how long a minute is. Remember, I told you once. One and two and three and—"

When they got to sixty by the slow count, Diane said, "Let's not. That only makes me see how draggy time can be."

"I'm going to sit down no matter what crawls over me." Vickie eased herself down as close to the door as possible.

Diane sat down too. After a moment her voice

104

came small and hesitant again in the darkness. "Vickie. Do you know any other verses? You know—from the Bible?"

Vickie shook her head and then, remembering that Diane could not see her head move, she said, "No," her voice sounding loud in the stillness.

"I just thought—maybe—maybe your dad read some to you."

"He has, but I don't remember any. Or—wait." She thought back to last summer. She remembered the papers in her father's desk when he had first started his search for God. And then she thought of the conversation that day with Pete when he had talked about the most important verse in the Bible. Suddenly, it was there, tucked away in her memory, safe. She said it slowly. "For God so loved the world, that He gave His only begotten Son, that whoever believes in Him should not perish, but have eternal life."

Diane did not say anything for a minute. Then, "Thanks, Vickie. I remember one other I've heard. It's the 'Children, obey your parents' one, but that's no help now. We should have thought of it sooner. But I suppose even if I had thought of it, it wouldn't have made any difference."

They sat in silence again, close together for warmth and comfort. Vickie made her mind count slowly, *One and two and three and,* to sixty and then start over again. Then she said, "On Christmas Eve when I was little, I used to say I couldn't wait for morning. My dad always said if I would just go to sleep the time would pass faster."

"I couldn't sleep now!" Diane exclaimed.

"Me either."

At that moment a noise on the other side of the door made them clutch each other and half rise. As they stared, the door opened to let in a crack of light. They stayed motionless, hardly daring to breathe as they waited, hoping to hear Mr. Montgomery's deep, "Vickie? Diane?"

Instead, there was only silence. Then they saw the door gradually open wider, scraping on the floor. No one was in sight as they looked out at the part of the kitchen visible through the narrow opening. They moved cautiously to the opening to peer out, blinking in the dim light that was so much brighter than the darkness they had sat in so long.

They still could not see anyone. Diane, behind Vickie, whispered, "Go on. Let's get out and run!"

They stooped to clear the low doorway and straightened up and then stopped abruptly, staring across the room at the two figures facing them in the kitchen doorway. A tall thin boy in ragged clothes, with long, uneven, black hair, and black eyes fixed threateningly on them, held a heavy stick upraised in his hand. A young girl pressed close to his side, her clothes as tattered as his, and her arms and legs like sticks. Her black hair hung in tangles around her thin cheeks, and her enormous black eyes were filled with fear.

The boy said something they did not understand as he took a step toward them, thrusting the girl behind him.

9

They backed away from him, holding the edge of the opened door, their eyes fixed on his thin face and angry stare. He said more words they could not understand.

Then Diane pointed as she sputtered, "Hey! You've got on my tennies!"

At the sound of Diane's voice, the girl looked down at the shoes too large for her small, narrow feet. The boy put his arm around the girl protectively and said something again. He brandished the heavy stick as he moved slowly toward them.

"I don't understand anything he says," Vickie whispered, not looking away from his face. "He's not talking English, is he?"

"I don't know. But I know one thing. They must be the ones who stole from your house, otherwise she wouldn't be wearing my tennies," Diane whispered back.

Vickie nodded, still carefully watching the boy's scowling face and upraised arm. "If only he'd put down that stick, I'd feel better. Let's smile and say something that sounds friendly."

"OK, you say it."

Vickie smiled as wide as possible. "Hi, how are you?" she said and heard her voice come out too loud.

But the boy shook his head and spit out sounds they could not understand. The girl crowded close to him, crying out something in a frightened voice, but he kept moving menacingly toward them.

"I think he's trying to back us into that room again. Careful, Diane. Get away from the door!"

The boy lunged at them, stick upraised, but they ducked out of his reach. Their backs against the wall, they inched slowly along away from the secret closet, not daring to look away from that angry face.

"If we can get out of the kitchen, we can run," Diane muttered out of the corner of her mouth.

Hearing Diane's voice, the boy darted a glance from one to the other and then swiftly moved back to stand by the kitchen doorway, blocking the way into the living room and the front door and escape.

"He knew we were trying to sneak past him. He's not going to let us out!"

Then a faint sound in the distance made the girls look at each other, hope springing in them. "That sounds like Bowser!"

"Let's hope my dad is with him!"

At the sound of the barking, close now, the girl cried quick, frightened words to the boy. He dropped the stick, grabbed her hand, and they raced out across the living room to the front door. Vickie and Diane raced after them just in time to see them disappear into the thick woods behind the house. The girls dashed down the dilapidated porch steps and stood in the weed-overgrown yard as Bowser burst through the trees and circled them, leaping and barking.

"Are we ever glad to see you!" Diane stooped and hugged him.

But Vickie looked beyond him to her parents who were running across the clearing toward them.

She felt ashamed, hating to face her father. But he crossed the clearing in huge strides and hugged her and then Diane. Mrs. Montgomery was right behind him, half laughing and half crying, anxiety mixed with reproach.

"What have you been doing all this time? Your clothes—your faces—your legs! You are caked with dirt! Oh, I'm so glad you're safe!"

Vickie looked at Diane and burst into laughter. Cobwebs clung to her curly hair, and dirt smudged black streaks across her forehead and down her cheeks. Her white shorts were black where she had rubbed against the wall and sat on the floor. But Diane was laughing too.

"If I look the way you do, I'm a mess!" Then Diane looked around. "It's still light. What time is it, anyway?"

"It's seven o'clock," Mrs. Montgomery answered. "You've been gone seven hours. Fortunately, I was so engrossed in my painting I wasn't aware of the time, so I didn't worry about you. I heard Bowser barking at the back door and was so impatient with him, I sent him off home. I didn't realize he was trying to tell me something. When I finally realized you were not home, I didn't know where to begin looking for you. I was just calling the forest ranger, but had not reached him, when your father came. He guessed right away where you might be. We left Francine and Pete at the house in case a message came there." She stopped her rush of words to draw a deep breath. "Now give an account of yourselves."

They both burst out, "We found the hiding

109

place! We know how to get in it. Come look."

They led the way through the house and into the kitchen. "See?"

Mrs. Montgomery crossed the room and bent to look into the dark closet. "Is *that* where you've been all afternoon? No wonder you're so dirty! But how? Why? You must have been terribly frightened."

They nodded, hearing the sympathy in her voice and feeling ashamed. They deserved a scolding instead of sympathy. Guilt lay heavy on Vickie as she faced her father's level gaze. His words were quiet, but his voice stern. "You have had a frightening experience. But you must remember that it happened because you disobeyed. I'm sorry about that. We'll face the consequences of that later. Just now, tell us what happened."

Vickie took a deep breath. "Well, we came in and found this small door standing open just a little way. We were curious to see what it looked like inside, so we stepped in just for a minute. And then all of a sudden the door shut on us."

"And we couldn't push it open from inside," Diane added.

While he listened, Mr. Montgomery examined the door, holding the open edge and running his fingers down the length of the door frame. "I knew there had to be *something* here," he muttered and felt slowly and carefully up and down along the edge of the door. "Ah—here it is. Feel here."

The girls pressed their fingers along the wood as he was doing.

110

"I don't feel anything."

"That's just it. You aren't supposed to. When the door is shut—" He slammed it as he spoke. "It looks like part of the wall. There is no knob or handle to show that it is a door."

"Dad! We wanted to show you what it's like inside."

"Yeah, Mr. Montgomery, now how can we get it open?"

"Press your fingers here," Mr. Montgomery answered.

"Where?" Diane felt the wall.

"Press hard. What happens?"

"Well—the wood—a piece of wood—a strip of wood moves. Goes in, sort of."

"Let me feel," Vickie begged.

"See what happens?" Mr. Montgomery asked. "That strip of wood is cleverly notched at several places so it will push in. That makes a groove for your fingers to fit in. Then you just pull the door. Pull hard."

"It won't move."

"Pull harder. There."

The door slowly creaked open a few inches. "How *neat*!" Diane exclaimed.

Mr. Montgomery looked at them. "Did you say the door was standing partway open when you got here?"

"Yes. Those kids must have found the secret of opening it, but how did they ever figure it—"

"What kids?" Mr. Montgomery asked.

"A boy and a girl who ran when they heard Bowser barking. They opened the door and let

111

us out. But they must have been the ones who shut us in, because otherwise they wouldn't have known that we were there."

"But even after they let us out, the boy kept threatening to hit us with a big stick," Diane chimed in. "They were talking, but we couldn't understand them. It sounded like—I don't know. Spanish, maybe."

Mr. Montgomery turned, his voice sharp. "Spanish?"

The girls looked at each other, and then Diane said, "I don't know. I'm just guessing. They both had real dark eyes and black hair."

"And the girl was skinnier than Diane."

"You mean they were young?"

"Oh, sure. The girl looked like she was about— what, Diane? Ten? Younger than either of us, anyway. But the boy was older."

"And guess what? She was wearing *my* sneakers, the ones missing from the closet."

"There, Carl. I knew whoever was in the house was not a real burglar, but just someone who needed help. We should find them. Where did they go?"

"They ran into the woods behind the house."

"If they've gone into the woods, they'll get lost," Mrs. Montgomery said in alarm.

But her husband shook his head. "I have an idea where we will be able to find them. I think they will be safe. Before we go home, I want to look inside this place."

"It's too dark to see much—oh." Vickie had not noticed that he had a flashlight. Her voice

112

was small and ashamed. "You thought you might have to look for us in the woods in the dark."

He nodded and hugged her. "I'm glad that was not necessary. Now I want a quick glimpse in here, even though I plan to return tomorrow for a closer examination and perhaps take some pictures."

He flashed on the strong light and stepped into the little room, the rest crowding behind him, feeling cramped in the confining space. The light showed the wooden sides and floor, thick with cobwebs and dirt.

"I was curious about this place. When we talked about what it might resemble, we compared it to a sod house. But I had my secretary look up in the encyclopedia a description of a sod house, and this does not fit. Sod houses were generally made by cutting sod—that is, blocks or sections of earth—into large brick-like pieces. The bricks were set in alternate rows to form walls. But a sod house was on top of the ground."

"But then what kind is this?"

"It's more on the order of a dugout, a house cut into the hillside, or down under the ground—"

"Oh," Diane exclaimed. "Like the ones they talked about in the *Little House on the Prairie* books. We should have remembered that."

"That's right. According to the description my secretary read, holes were dug out of the hillside and then wood poles or sometimes canvas formed the walls and ceiling. Often the floor was packed earth that could be swept and even washed."

"I told the girls they're using the same idea to

make rather elaborate underground homes now to conserve energy. They are supposed to be cool in the summer and warm in the winter."

"I believe it," Vickie exclaimed. "We were pretty cold in there today."

Mr. Montgomery flashed his light around again. "Assuming this was built as a refuge for escaping slaves, the builder had a compassionate heart. He tried to make it as safe as possible."

"But, Carl, that would have been a hundred years ago and more. You think it's been hidden away here all this time?"

"I can only speculate, of course, but I think it could have been used in later years as a pantry. A cool place to keep vegetables the way people used to have root cellars."

He turned toward the door. "It is going to be interesting to find out who discovered how to open the door."

"Dad! There's something else. We think those kids were staying here. We're sure the blankets on the beds aren't old like everything else is. Come and look." Vickie pushed open the bedroom door and stopped. "They're gone! The blankets are gone!"

Mr. Montgomery stood looking past them into the room. "You didn't see anyone else but the two children?"

"No, nobody."

"Carl, I think we had better get these girls home so they can get cleaned up and eat dinner. It's getting dark, and Francine and Pete will begin to worry about us, even with that good flashlight."

"Remember, we do have the girls' marked trees to follow back." Mr. Montgomery grinned at them as he closed the door firmly.

They followed single file through the dark woods they had crashed through so many hours before, Bowser staying close to them this time. Vickie wondered if Diane, like herself, was feeling relief that they were safe, but shame at her parents' welcome of them without any scolding.

Diane answered her thought by whispering, "I'd feel better if your dad got mad and bawled us out."

"He will," Vickie answered. "I don't mean he will bawl us out, exactly, but he will talk to us about it. And I'm sure he will punish us some way."

"Maybe if we tell him we're really, really sorry—"

Vickie shook her head. "That's not enough. He says people always find it easy to say they're sorry, but that doesn't wipe out the wrong they did."

"Doesn't he ever defend anyone who's guilty of something?"

Vickie's head shake was even more positive. "Never. He doesn't defend anyone unless he's convinced they're not guilty. He's always been that way. You know how he hates it when someone tells a lie."

"Don't I know! I still remember how strict he was when he talked to me the time—you know— the time I pretended I took the bracelets." Diane stopped and then in a small voice said, "I guess while we're on the subject, I'd better be honest and call it what your dad did, and say the time I *lied* about stealing the bracelets."

"His standards are kind of hard to live with, even when you know he's right."

They plodded along the sandy shore behind the Montgomerys, who were walking hand in hand.

"I wonder how your dad knows, or thinks he knows, where to find those kids?"

Vickie stopped so abruptly that Diane collided with her. "I bet I know. They're at the ranger station! Remember how positive I was that someone was in that room?"

"Vickie! Why would those dirty kids be there? They acted—well, wild. How would he know them? Why would he hide them?"

"Let's catch up and ask."

They raced along the beach and caught up just as they reached the house. "Dad," Vickie asked, out of breath, "are you going to see the forest ranger? Is that where you think those kids are?"

"Yes." He looked at her in surprise. "How did you guess?"

"Because yesterday when we were there, I saw—"

Before she could finish, the screen door burst open and Francine rushed down the steps to hug Vickie and ruffle Diane's curls. "I'm so glad to see you! You had us so worried. Ugh—you're filthy! Get in the shower. You must be starved. Come on in. Dinner's been simmering for the last couple of hours."

116

Pete grinned down at them from the top step. "Now that you're safe, I'll admit that I'm glad you were temporarily lost. It means we'll all get a terrific meal out of it. Francine's cooked up a storm here to welcome you back." He waved his hand toward the table set near the windows with candles and flowers. "I warned her to fix a double batch of everything, so we'd get some as well as you two starving refugees."

His tone was bantering, but Vickie caught the undertone of worry that laced it.

She and Diane looked at each other, and then she said, "We really shouldn't get such nice treatment. We should be sent to bed without supper." Her voice quavered as she looked at their faces and then quickly away. "We're sorry we disobeyed, Dad."

"I'm the one who should get all the punishment, Mr. Montgomery. I kept pestering Vickie about going back to the house and she kept saying no, because you said not to. And then I—well, I went anyway. I think Vickie came along just to be sure I would be all right."

"Is that so, Vickie?"

Vickie heard her father's quiet question, and hesitated, digging at the ground with her foot. Finally she shook her head. "Not really. I talked myself into believing that since Bowser was along, it wasn't the same as going back alone, which you said not to do. But—I would have gone anyway."

"We know you're sorry, but that does not wipe out the disobedience."

"I'm *never* going to disobey again," Diane burst out.

Mr. Montgomery looked down at her, a smile tugging at his lips as he heard the determination in her voice. Then his voice became serious as he shook his head. "You can't do it alone, Diane. You need God's help for that."

He pulled the girls to him for a quick hug and then started up the stairs. "Let's talk this over later after we've eaten and feel better. And tomorrow we'll go over and talk to the forest ranger."

But Mrs. Montgomery said, "Carl, should you wait that long? I'm worried about those children out in the woods. Who are they?"

He stood frowning in thought. Then, without answering her question, he looked across at Francine. "Will your fancy dinner wait another hour or so?"

"It will, but I'm not sure Pete will." She smiled at him, and then said, "Since we were not sure when you would be back, I fixed something that could be reheated a couple of times if necessary."

"Good." Mr. Montgomery reached to push the screen door open. "If the rest of you want to go ahead and eat—" he began.

But the girls begged, "Dad!" and, "Can't we go too, Mr. Montgomery?"

"I am going also," Mrs. Montgomery said firmly.

"All right. You win. I suppose it really would not be fair to you not to let you see this mystery

118

through. I will wait while you girls get an apple or a sandwich. Then come along."

"You grubby kids get off some of that dirt while I make you a sandwich to eat on the way," Francine ordered.

As the girls started into the house, Vickie heard her father say something in a low voice and heard her mother's startled, "Really? But so far north? Do you think they're by themselves?"

The rest of what they said was lost to her as they went outside, the screen door slamming behind them. By the time the girls yanked open the car doors to pile into the back seat, Mr. Montgomery had the engine going.

It was dark as they flashed past trees—the headlights of the car barely lighted the blacktopped road. Mr. Montgomery slowed the car, saying, "I never like to drive up to the speed limit on these dark roads even when there is not a great deal of traffic. I'm always afraid some little terrified wild animal will dart out of the woods, and I would not be able to stop in time."

"Those kids sure looked like wild things, especially the little girl, didn't she, Diane? I can feel sorry for her now that I'm not so scared and now that her brother isn't waving a big stick at us. Do you suppose they live around here?"

Mr. Montgomery only shook his head without answering as he slowed to turn onto the gravel drive leading to the small brick house where lights shone from front windows. As the car lights swept across the house and the car crunched on

119

the gravel, a light in a side window went out abruptly.

Mr. Montgomery shut off the motor and turned toward the girls. "I want to handle this very carefully, because I'm only guessing at answers to questions I have. In fact, I'm really guessing at the questions at this point. So please let me do the talking unless I ask you for your contribution. Understand?"

His voice was so stern that the girls nodded wordlessly.

They followed him along the narrow sidewalk to the door and listened to his knock. After a few moments the door opened, and the ranger blocked the entrance, looking at them. The light from the room behind him shone on his black hair. He was out of uniform, dressed in gray slacks and a red sport shirt.

His white teeth flashed in a smile as he said, "Why, hello. Mr. Montgomery, isn't it? What can I do for you?"

"May we come in a minute?"

"Certainly." He stepped to one side, nodding his head politely to Mrs. Montgomery when she was introduced. He looked at the girls, his eyes unfriendly. But when he looked back at Mr. Montgomery, he moved his mouth into a smile and waited.

They all looked expectantly at Mr. Montgomery who gazed steadily at the ranger. "Mr. Alvarez, I want you to know that I am here only as a private citizen, not in any official capacity. I must tell you that I am a lawyer, and therefore am familiar with the laws of the country. However, I am not here this evening in a legal capacity either."

The ranger nodded, his eyes darting nervously from one to the other and then back to Mr. Montgomery. "Yes, your daughter mentioned the other day that you are a lawyer."

"You have some knowledge of the law yourself, of course."

Vickie, listening to her father's kind and courteous voice, wondered what all this was leading up to. Why didn't he just burst out, as she wanted to, and ask, "Are those kids here?"

Then Mr. Montgomery said, "I believe the girls mentioned you came from southern California?"

Though it was not actually a question, it sounded like one. The ranger nodded, running his tongue quickly over his lips. "I said California, but, yes, it was the southern part."

"What nationality are you?"

The ranger stood straight, and his voice was belligerent as he answered, "American. I'm a United States citizen!"

"Of course. You would have to be a citizen to be in this job. But I'm asking what your nationality is. I believe Mexican?"

The ranger's eyes narrowed and his mouth hardened as he snapped. "Yes. Is this prejudice I'm facing?"

"Not at all," Mr. Montgomery answered quickly. "The question seemed necessary to give me some background information. It confirms an assumption I have made concerning events that have taken place in the past few days."

Then with an odd note of pity and sadness in his voice, he said, "Would you please tell us about the two young people you have been hiding for several days?"

"I don't know what you are talking about." He gestured. "There's no room here to hide anyone."

The girls looked at the closed door across the room and then back at the ranger who stared defiantly at Mr. Montgomery. His arms were folded as he leaned back, half sitting on a table.

But Mr. Montgomery shook his head, his face showing sympathy. "You really must not hide them any longer. You know the girls have seen them, so denying that they exist is futile."

"I can't keep tabs on everybody who walks through the woods—"

"You should. It's your job!" Mr. Montgomery's stern tone softened as he continued, "Apparently the children knew about the old house in the woods. Did they stumble on it accidentally, or did you show it to them? And did they discover the secret room by themselves?"

The ranger frowned and shot a puzzled, questioning look at the girls. But to Mr. Montgomery he said, "You seem to have imagined a mystery."

"It is a mystery, and one I hope we can resolve in the best way for all who are caught up in it. One of the pieces of the mystery is connected with the secret room in the old house. That narrow place was a refuge in past years for some who were escaping injustice. Your children were frightened when our girls came exploring in the old house this afternoon. Because they were frightened, they shut the girls in the hiding place."

The ranger gave a start of surprise, his eyes shifting to the closed door across the room and then quickly back. But he insisted, "I don't know about a secret room in any house."

Mr. Montgomery ignored the remark as he went on calmly, "Later, apparently they were sorry and let the girls out, and we are grateful for that. Now we would like to help them—and you."

He stopped, his gaze steady on the ranger's face, and his voice stern as he added, "I believe certain laws are being broken, and that is always dangerous. I would advise you to confide in me, Mr. Alvarez, and let me see if I can help."

"You talk about obeying the law," the ranger snapped. "Do you have a search warrant to come in this way?"

"Oh, please!" Mrs. Montgomery moved suddenly to put her hand gently on his arm. "Our girls said they looked so hungry and worn. Please let us help them!"

The ranger stood rigid, not looking at her, not answering. Vickie wanted to run across the room and throw open the door. But she did not dare. This was something her father had to handle, and he had warned them not to interfere.

She listened as her father answered the ranger's question. "I would like to handle this without resorting to warrants and arrests. All I need is your cooperation."

Mrs. Montgomery stepped between them, her

red-gold hair shining in the light, her blue eyes flashing, her sweet, light voice indignant. "Here we stand talking, while two ragged, hungry, frightened children need help."

Before the ranger could stop her, she stepped quickly across the room and pulled open the door, reaching to find the light switch. As light flooded the room, they could see the boy and girl standing close together, facing them. The boy had one arm around the girl's trembling figure. The other was upraised, his hand clutching a knife, its long slender blade clearly outlined. His glittering black eyes were fixed on Mrs. Montgomery.

10

Vickie stood hardly breathing as she saw her mother smile at the wild-looking boy, her hand out in a gentle appeal. Then the ranger barked a short explosive word, and the boy looked at him. The ranger crossed the room in quick strides and gently released the boy's grip on the knife, talking to him in a soothing tone.

Vickie felt herself trembling with relief as the ranger came slowly back toward them, his head down and his shoulders sagging. He turned to look at the two figures still huddled together and said something to them in the same soft, lilting tone he had used to the boy. They stared back at him and then, moving slowly past Mrs. Montgomery, the girl hanging tightly to the boy's arm, they sidled over and crouched close together in a corner of the sofa across the room from Vickie and Diane.

The ranger slumped at the table, resting his elbows on the top and putting his hands over his face in a tired gesture. After a moment, talking through his fingers, he said, "I guess down deep I'm glad it's over. Glad you've caught up with us. I just—just feel sorry for the poor kids."

"Can you tell us about it?" Mr. Montgomery asked in his kind voice as he sat down opposite the ranger.

Mrs. Montgomery motioned the girls to chairs near where she sat as close to the scared children as she dared. Vickie felt her legs trembling from release of tension and from tiredness.

The ranger folded his hands in front of him on the table. "Well, as you've guessed, I suppose, they're Mexican aliens—illegal aliens." He jerked his head in their direction. "They are brother and sister, all that's left of a family of ten." He stopped, struggling to steady his voice.

"What happened to the rest?"

"Their father was desperate to get better living conditions for his family in America. The place they thought was the land of hope." The ranger's voice was bitter, and at the harsh sound the boy half rose, his face mirroring fear.

He sank back as the ranger gestured at him and went on. "How they raised enough money to come, I don't know. They must have sold everything they possessed and borrowed whatever they could. They planned this carefully, and about a month ago they crossed the border at night by wading in the river. At places the water was up to the girl's neck. They headed for a spot just across the border where they would meet two men—'nice Americans'—who would get them out of Texas and up to a neutral place in the north. There they expected to find work and, they hoped, not be noticed. They paid a hundred dollars apiece, including the six-month old baby, for safety. That's one thousand dollars."

He stopped to bite his lip and rub his hands together. "They were picked up at the border in a U-Haul, crowded in with a dozen other people. Then they ran into trouble. The Border Patrol had been alerted—I suspect by the two nice Americans they had trusted. They had to hide. Instead of the trip in the U-Haul taking two days, it took a week—part of the time they hid on side roads. They never even got out of Texas. They had no water, no food. The sun in Texas in July is murder. Inside that U-Haul—they pounded—begged to be let out—"

His voice broke, and he buried his face in his hands again. Vickie saw tears seeping through his fingers and felt them splashing down her face and knew Diane and her mother were crying, too.

"When they finally opened the truck, only four people were alive. Two men and—" He gestured. "These two."

Mr. Montgomery got up to stare unseeing out the window into the darkness. Without turning around, his voice husky, he asked, "How did they get here?"

"They got here through sheer terror!" The ranger stood up violently, knocking over his chair. Once again the boy jumped to his feet. The girl cried out words and clung to his hand. Mrs. Montgomery turned swiftly and knelt beside her, her arm gently circling the bony figure that shrank away.

The ranger stood, hands thrust deep in his pockets. "Look at them! What harm would they do anyone if they stayed here? She's ten. He's fourteen. They're all alone in a strange country. They don't know the language. They've got no money. If they're turned in, they'll be sent back. To what? They've got nothing back home either. They've got no home. No family. Nothing. Sure

I helped them. Yes, I'm Mexican, same as they are. But more than that, I'm a human being and so are they!"

He sat down, exhausted. After a moment he went on in a quieter voice. "I don't know how they got this far. I haven't pressed them for details. I haven't wanted to make them relive what must have been a nightmare."

He flicked a scornful glance at the girls. "Sure they stole. But only what they were desperate for. You can spare a little grub, can't you? And a pair of old run-down sneakers?"

Vickie glanced at Diane who sat staring at the floor, twisting her hands together, and Vickie realized that her own hands were gripped so tightly together that they ached.

Mr. Montgomery sat down at the table. "Did you know them before they came here?"

The ranger looked away. "No." His voice was loudly defiant.

Mr. Montgomery looked back steadily, his voice soft yet blunt as he said, "There must be some reason why they came here instead of staying in Texas or going to a closer state, perhaps California. How did they just happen to find you?"

Vickie heard the insistent note in her father's voice. She watched the ranger bite his lip and shift uncomfortably, his eyes avoiding Mr. Montgomery's steady gaze.

Then his shoulders slumped and he nodded, blurting out words. "My fiancée knew about this family. She gave them my name and address and directions to get here by bus. She wanted them to get as far north as possible, away from any chance of being traced and sent back. She wanted the children to have a chance for a better life."

Vickie looked at the boy who half rose at the anger in the ranger's voice. His eyes flashed from one to the other as the men spoke, following the words though not their meaning.

The ranger's voice was loud and angry as he went on. "So, not knowing what else to do, they hid out and gradually worked their way north. I don't know how. Hitchhiked some, maybe. Walked. They saved the little money they had to come the last part by bus. My fiancée had sent the father instructions with names of cities and the bus line. The boy has a paper with the words copied down. I've been checking bus arrivals for days, not knowing what had happened to the family, but afraid—"

"How would these two know how to find you, not knowing English?"

"I tell you I don't know all those details! They knew my name, the name of the town, my job—at least the father did. And my name is on the paper the boy has folded in a tiny square in his pocket. Apparently when they got off the bus they just began walking along the road, hoping somehow to find me, but not daring to ask for help."

"Tell us how you found them," Mrs. Montgomery urged, her soft voice filled with pity.

The ranger took a deep breath. "I spotted that smoke last Sunday and wondered if it could possibly be a sign of these children."

129

He looked at Mr. Montgomery. "OK, I lied to you about the smoke. But I wanted to buy a little time for these two. I had found them that Sunday, half dead from hunger and exhaustion and fear. They were trying to cook a meal over an open fire. Sure—food they stole from the grocery store, because they hadn't eaten for two days. I had to figure some way to help them. That old house is a terrible place to make a couple of terrified kids stay. But I couldn't keep them with me all the time."

He looked at the girls, his voice lined with bitterness. "You weren't very welcome that day you came. They were here trying to clean up a little, and I had to send them back to the old house before they had had a chance to wash their clothes."

Vickie looked at Diane and knew she felt miserable too, remembering the dirty bedroom, the narrow, hard cots, no running water, no lights at night to make bearable the sound of mice skittering across bare dusty floors.

"So it was a shock to you and to them when the girls discovered the house?" Mr. Montgomery prompted.

The ranger nodded and then frowned. "I don't know anything about a secret room. Since I am new here, I don't know much about that old place. In fact, I was surprised the first time I saw it. But, what about the secret room? What was its purpose?"

"A hundred years and more ago it was a hideaway for slaves escaping north."

The ranger's mouth twisted bitterly. "Still

130

needed today, isn't it? People are still looking for freedom, for safety—and not finding it."

Then he shook his head. "No, they didn't mention the room to me. You say they shut the girls into it? When?"

He turned to the boy without waiting for an answer and asked a question. Words poured from the boy, and the ranger nodded as he listened. He looked at Mr. Montgomery. "He said they were in the house when the three of you were there yesterday—no, the day before—"

"Where were they? We didn't see them," Diane burst out.

"They heard you coming and ran up to the second floor. Then when you went into the kitchen, Juan slipped down and listened behind the living room door. He couldn't understand what you were saying, but he could hear and see you pounding and pushing along the wall. Juan is a very clever boy—he wouldn't have survived this long if he weren't. He figured if you were interested in something on that wall, he should be too. So he looked until he found how to open the door."

More words poured suddenly from the boy. The ranger listened, interrupting occasionally to ask other questions. "He had just discovered it, had just pulled it open when the girls came back today—"

"I said I felt eyes watching us!" Vickie exclaimed.

"Juan was alone. He panicked and shut the door on you. I think Juan would like to have left you there. But when he told the little sister later,

131

she begged him to let you out. Young as she is, she knows what it means to be shut in, to be a prisoner through no fault of her own."

Vickie looked at the girl's thin, still frightened face and then at her father. She wanted him to say, "We'll help them escape. We'll hide them."

But she knew he would not. The law said aliens had to be deported. She remembered the loud, angry discussion one day in social studies—the class had argued heatedly when the teacher said the law had to be obeyed even if the innocent suffered. Dad believed in the law. He was a lawyer and believed if you were guilty of something, you had to pay the penalty.

She watched as he put both hands flat on the table, leaning forward, facing the ranger, and asked, "Do you believe in God?"

The ranger jerked his head to stare at Mr. Montgomery. "God? Yes. No. What's He got to do with this?"

Mr. Montgomery's voice was clear. "I am a lawyer, sworn to uphold the law." He raised a silencing hand when the ranger muttered, "Lawyers can be bribed!"

"Yes, I admit that. Some can be. But I am not one of them. I am an honest man before other men. But most of all, I am an honest man before the God I have recently come to accept as the One who rules my life. He has given His rules in a Book that says the one who breaks the law must be judged by the law—"

"So you're going to turn them over—send them back to nothing."

Vickie half stood, wanting to burst out, "Dad! Can't we do something for them? Find someone to adopt them?" She could tell by Diane's tense figure and clenched hands that she wanted to ask the same thing.

But Mr. Montgomery was going on in his quiet, controlled voice. "I have always believed that justice must be tempered with mercy. And I have found that the God who judges is also the God who shows mercy by forgiving."

The room was so quiet that Vickie could hear leaves rustling outside the open window in the soft night. She saw the hope that sprang in the ranger's face. He straightened. "So what are you going to do?"

Mr. Montgomery looked at the brother and sister sitting motionless and cramped on the narrow sofa, their eyes fixed uncomprehendingly on him. Vickie had watched as they looked back and forth, following the sound of the voices but not understanding the words.

She noticed that her mother had moved back to her chair. With a quick movement, Vickie got up and stepped over beside the girl, sitting beside her on the sofa arm, her hand reaching to take hold of the thin, nervous fingers. The girl shrank back, glancing up at Vickie fearfully. Then her hand tightened on Vickie's until she was clinging to it desperately.

Mr. Montgomery watched Vickie's impulsive movement and then picked up the thread of what he had been saying. "Since this is the weekend, it is difficult to do anything of a legal nature. We will use the two days to get the children cleaned and fed and into some decent clothes. Then on Monday you and they will go back to the city with me—"

The ranger stood, his voice harsh again, and once more the girl cowered back from the violent movement her brother made as he, too, stood. "You can't turn them in! What mercy is there in that? You know what will happen to them."

"You have no choice!"

Vickie stared at her father. She had never heard his voice with such a sound of steel flashing in it.

"I am offering you the only possible solution that will make it easy for the two children. Sit down and listen!"

The ranger stood immobile, glaring back at Mr. Montgomery. Then he gestured toward the boy, and they both sat down reluctantly.

"We will go back to the city for a deportation hearing—" The ranger made another protesting movement, but stopped at the steely order, "Wait!"

"They must be reported to the United States Immigration and Naturalization Services of the Department of Justice. Remember—they are illegal aliens. Legally they can be sent back even if it means going back to nothing. That's the law."

Vickie sat tensely, conscious that her fingers were gripping the girl's hand tightly, and that the girl was clinging as hard to her hand.

"There are two steps we can take. One is to find the men operating this illegal smuggling ring and have them prosecuted—"

The ranger shrugged. "You do that and you cut off the only means these people have to escape their wretched life."

"What kind of escape is it for them to pay every cent they can beg and borrow to get here and, if they survive, to run and hide and take the lowest paying jobs and live always with the fear of discovery?" Mr. Montgomery's voice crackled with anger.

When the ranger did not reply, he went on. "After we have reported the children, we will enter a plea that they be adopted to keep them from being deported."

Hope sprang again into the ranger's face. "Is—is that possible? You mean you—you—" He looked from Mr. Montgomery to his wife and back again.

Mr. Montgomery shook his head. "No, not adopted by us. They would feel strange with us. But I believe I can find a home for them."

He stopped and turned to look sympathetically at the brother and sister, his arm protectively around her as she clung to him. "A home for them *both* so they can stay together. But we do it my way—legally," he repeated.

The ranger stood, reaching to grasp Mr. Montgomery's hand, his voice choked with emotion as he struggled to form words of thanks. Then he turned to the boy and girl and spoke rapidly, words pouring out in soft, musical sounds. Vickie watched the expression on the boy's face turn from hard suspicion and anger to disbelief and then to hope as the meaning of what the ranger said became clear to him. He struggled to speak, his lips quivering. Then suddenly he put his hands over his face and sat down on the sofa, sobs shaking him. Broken words came and the ranger explained. "He is embarrassed to cry. It is just that—it has been hard. He has been so fearful for his little sister."

He stopped and looked around at them, Vickie and Diane both in tears, Mrs. Montgomery with tears in her eyes, and Mr. Montgomery with his handkerchief in his hand.

The ranger touched the boy's shoulder and gestured at them all. The boy stood up and went over to stand in front of Mr. Montgomery. "I—pay—back."

The ranger explained, "He knows the word *pay*. It is the one word aliens hear all the time. 'You pay,' they are told. They know nothing is free."

"Tell him he is not to think of that now. We need to pay him back for what other Americans took from him—his family."

Mr. Montgomery's voice was grim, and at the sound the boy shrank back, looking at the ranger. He quickly said something that stilled the fear that had leaped once more to the boy's eyes.

Mr. Montgomery pulled money from his wallet and handed it to the ranger. "This should buy them some new clothes and—" He looked at the boy. "And a haircut."

"And you want them ready to go with you Monday?"

Mr. Montgomery had turned toward the door, but stopped at the question, his hand on the doorknob. He looked back over his shoulder. "A few more days won't matter. Let's give them a chance to rest and get over their fright. Vickie and Diane could use some Spanish lessons to keep them busy and out of mischief. They've been pretty keyed up these last few days. Anyway, I am supposed to be on vacation for another week."

He smiled as he pulled open the door and nodded back at the ranger's fervent, "Thank you, sir."

Vickie followed Diane into the back seat, sitting on the edge and leaning forward with her arms folded on the back of the front seat.

"I can't believe the way this has turned out! We never thought when we saw that smoke last Sunday that all this was going to happen."

"Poor children. Think how afraid they must have been." Mrs. Montgomery's soft voice was troubled.

"I will have to admit that it was a good thing you did see the smoke and kept pestering me about it. Otherwise they would have kept running until they were caught and sent back. In a sense I suppose you could say the smoke was a signal, even though they did not intend it to be."

"I still want to know how they made that noise that scared us away the first time we saw the house. And how they could have been in the house at the same time we were and we never saw them."

Vickie turned to look at Diane who sat huddled in one corner of the back seat, staring out into the night. She suddenly realized how quiet Diane had been all during the scene in the ranger's house. Ordinarily she would be bouncing now with excitement, full of plans of how they would help the brother and sister learn some English in the next few days—and eager to pick up enough Spanish to show off at school next month. Yet now she sat crouched in the corner, not saying a word.

Vickie look at her anxiously. Diane was not strong enough yet to stand all the swimming and biking and running around they had been doing since Sunday. The doctor kept warning her that she had to take it easy and not try to do everything everyone else did. And now she had gone ever since noon without much to eat. She knew how ravenous she was, and knew Diane must be too.

"You OK, Diane?"

Diane's head nodded.

"You don't feel sick?"

"Uh-uh."

She still did not turn from staring out into the dark night.

"I hope Pete didn't eat up everything. I'm starved. How about you?"

"Uh-huh."

Understanding then came to Vickie, and she leaned over to whisper, "Don't worry about my dad being mad at us. Sure—he's going to see to it that we remember we disobeyed him. Maybe he'll make us write a hundred times, 'I will never prowl around deserted houses again.'"

She tried to make it a joke and knew she had failed when Diane turned to her suddenly, her voice low and broken.

138

"Vickie, don't you see? All my life I've been feeling sorry for myself. All my life I've thought how hard I had it because my father walked out on me. And because my mother is so—so bitter that she—she drinks and can't say nice things about anyone. All my life I've thought everyone else had it easy but me. I've—I've even been mad at you lots of times inside because you live in such a ha-happy f-family. And then—now—tonight—that girl—only two of them left out of a whole family, wandering all around scared to death, afraid even of us—"

She stopped, wiping tears from her cheeks with her fingers, her voice cracking as she whispered, "I just feel so ashamed."

Vickie sat helpless, not knowing how to comfort her as the car crunched over the graveled driveway and stopped.

Mr. Montgomery looked at them in the rear-view mirror. "I believe the first order of business is to get that dinner that Francine has been saving—I hope—for us."

But Diane moved suddenly and said, "Mr. Montgomery. Could I—could I talk to you a minute?"

"Of course. Louise, you and Vickie go in and let Francine and Pete know we are back. Diane, come up here in the front."

Vickie followed her mother into the house and rushed into the bedroom, brushing past Francine's questions. She went into the bathroom to wash her face and comb her hair, doing it mechanically. But all the time her mind kept seeing Diane's huddled figure and then hearing her desperate, "Could I talk to you, please?"

She went back through the kitchen to the porch and heard her mother's warm, sympathetic voice telling about the brother and sister, and Francine's exclamations of pity. As she helped bring food to the table and pour water into the glasses, she glanced out the window. The car dome light was on. In its glow she saw her father holding his small Bible in his hand, the Bible that was never far from him. She saw Diane nodding at what he was saying.

Vickie looked quickly away, her throat tightening, afraid of what was happening in the car. Then the sound of a door slamming shut cut across her mother's voice. They all looked toward the screen door as Mr. Montgomery opened it, and Diane stepped in shyly, a soft smile on her thin face and a happy light in her eyes.

Before Diane said anything, Vickie knew what she would say. "Guess what? I just said that I want Jesus to be my Savior, like John three sixteen says."

Then she yanked out the chair at the table beside Vickie and whispered, "I'll tell you all about it after supper. Right now, I'm starved!"

Vickie looked at the bright glow of Diane's face, and anger washed over her in a hot flood. She had thought they shared everything. But now Diane had crossed an invisible line into another world. *She's left me behind!*

Diane had a gladness Vickie did not know anything about. It was the same gladness her father

140

had. The two of them were together in it. She looked at Pete who was smiling happily at Diane. Maybe he had the gladness too. That left Francine and her mother and herself. *This is what it feels like to be an alien.*

Vickie stared down at her plate, not wanting to see Diane's happiness. A whole year they had shared experiences, laughed at the same things, sometimes cried over things. Now that was all changed.

She felt her mother's light touch on her arm and looked up. "Remember," her mother's eyes seemed to say. "Remember what I told you. Be a friend Diane can always count on. Be glad she is happy."

She looked at her mother uncertainly and then listened to Diane. Her usual sparkle and bounce were back as she told Pete and Francine about their first wild dash back through the woods from the house, forgetting the signals they had tied to the trees. And about their feelings when they were shut in the cramped, cold room.

She had learned through the year that Diane used the sparkle as a cover for the hurts and disappointments in her life. Now the sparkle seemed to just bubble from inside.

Vickie looked back at her mother and smiled. She hoped her eyes sent back the message, "I *am* glad Diane is happy."

But she did not want her mother—or anyone—to know the question that kept asking itself inside her. Who else was going to be touched by this new belief that made her father and Diane show happiness in a way they never had before? She only knew she wasn't ready for it herself. Not yet.